She Was Made For Motherhood.

The thought didn't surprise Jack. But what did catch him off guard was the deep longing for this intimate family scene to be his. He watched as Frannie stood near her small fireplace with the baby in her arms. She was looking down into the tiny face, speaking in a quiet, earnest tone.

She loved babies—that was certain—and she seemed to love his baby in particular.

"I wish I could find someone who would care for her like you do while I'm at work."

"You can't possibly keep taking her to work with you."

"I don't have a choice. Unless you've changed your mind about keeping her?"

She hesitated. "I suppose I could keep her until a space in a reputable day-care facility becomes available."

"Are you sure? I don't want to take advantage of you." *At least, not in the baby-sitting department....*

Dear Reader,

Welcome to a new year with Silhouette Desire! We begin the year in celebration—it's the 10th Anniversary of MAN OF THE MONTH! And kicking off the festivities is the incomparable Diana Palmer, with January's irresistible hero, Simon Hart, in *Beloved*.

Also launching this month is Desire's series FORTUNE'S CHILDREN: THE BRIDES. So many of you wrote to us that you loved Silhouette's series FORTUNE'S CHILDREN—now here's a whole new branch of the family! Award-winning author Jennifer Greene inaugurates this series with *The Honor Bound Groom*.

Popular Anne Marie Winston begins BUTLER COUNTY BRIDES, a new miniseries about three small-town friends who find true love, with *The Baby Consultant*. Sara Orwig offers us a marriage of convenience in *The Cowboy's Seductive Proposal*. Next, experience love on a ranch in *Hart's Baby* by Christy Lockhart. And opposites attract in *The Scandalous Heiress* by Kathryn Taylor.

So, indulge yourself in 1999 with Silhouette Desire—powerful, provocative and passionate love stories that speak to today's multifaceted woman. Each month we offer you six compelling romances to meet your many moods, with heroines you'll care about and heroes to die for. Silhouette Desire is everything *you* desire in a romance novel.

Enjoy!

Joan Marlow Golan
Senior Editor, Silhouette Desire

Please address questions and book requests to:
Silhouette Reader Service
U.S.: 3010 Walden Ave., P.O. Box 1325, Buffalo, NY 14269
Canadian: P.O. Box 609, Fort Erie, Ont. L2A 5X3

THE BABY CONSULTANT
ANNE MARIE WINSTON

SILHOUETTE *Desire*
Published by Silhouette Books
America's Publisher of Contemporary Romance

SILHOUETTE BOOKS

ISBN 0-373-76191-0

THE BABY CONSULTANT

Copyright © 1999 by Anne Marie Rodgers

Printed in U.S.A.

ANNE MARIE WINSTON

has believed in happy endings all her life. Having the opportunity to share them with her readers gives her great joy. Anne Marie enjoys figure skating and working in the gardens of her south-central Pennsylvania home.

To Ruth Ann, my "forever friend."

We've shared Barbies and babies,
Harlequins and hospital rooms,
Pregnancies and "pigs."
Thanks for the wonderful memories.

One

He wasn't gorgeous, as Dee had led her to believe. His nose looked as if it had been rearranged by someone even bigger than he; his eyes were an unremarkable gray. Clean shaven and well-defined, his jaw thrust forward just a shade shy of pugnacious while his light brown, almost-but-not-quite-blond hair was cut military-short along the sides, curling only at the top where it had escaped the razor's forays.

Still, she could see the appeal. She studied him as he spoke into the phone he held to his ear while he paced back and forth at the far end of his office. His shoulders were broad enough to set a tea service on. He was taller than any of her brothers, maybe six-one, with long, long legs and a wide, straight back that tapered to a trim waist. And his butt was to die for. She almost laughed aloud. She would never have thought of that phrase before she'd moved away from home and found a life of her own.

Then he turned and smiled at her.

Frannie set down her purse and briefcase and took a seat

in the chair across from Jack Ferris's desk. Actually, she had no choice. That smile virtually took her breath away, weakened her knees, made her heart pound—every stupid cliché she'd ever heard suddenly didn't seem so stupid.

Dee had warned her: "Women fight over him. Literally."

Unbelievable. One little shift of expression, one flash of white teeth and a penetrating personal moment of eye contact...she'd probably fetch his slippers and pipe if he smiled at her like that again.

"He'll be with you in a moment." The receptionist with the disgustingly gorgeous figure and the perfect teeth smiled sweetly at Frannie before closing the door of the office. It figured. She would have bet good green bucks that this man would hire help that looked like something out of a sports magazine's annual swimsuit issue. It would have been easy to hate her if she hadn't been so nice.

He was still talking on the telephone, one hand splayed across his hip in what looked like exasperation. "I said I'm sorry, Mona. I have a game that day or you know I'd love to take you." His voice oozed smooth honey, but Frannie doubted that Mona would think he was so charming if she could see the way he was practically gritting his teeth. It was obvious he didn't want to do whatever the woman at the other end was trying to rope him into.

Deliberately trying not to eavesdrop, she pulled her briefcase onto her lap and extracted the portfolio of her work she'd brought along. Flipping it open, she forgot about Jack Ferris and his famous charm. With a critical eye, she studied the photos of some of the wedding dresses she'd made. That cream satin one had such nice pearl work and embroidered detail on the bodice—she should have taken a shot from the front as well as the back. The ruffled Chantilly lace on the chapel-length train was gorgeous, if she did say so herself. And the Victorian...not her style, but it had looked lovely on the girl for whom she'd made it, with its leg-o'-mutton sleeves. The girl had pinned her hair up loosely and forsaken a veil for a stately plumed hat Frannie had suggested, which should have looked ridiculous but didn't. And here was that darling silk sheath with a yoke of alençon lace. She'd enjoyed making that one. But perhaps she should have brought all traditional styles along. That was what most brides wanted, she'd discovered, and if she was considering placing some of them in a brochure—oh, bother. Wasn't that why she was here? So this highly recommended ad agency could tell her what would be best?

As she shuffled through the photos again, the telephone's small beep told her that the consultant was off the phone.

"Miss Brooks. I apologize for the delay. I'm Jack Ferris." He advanced across the room with three long strides, hand outstretched and that intimate smile projected full blast at her.

It was impossible not to respond. She half rose to meet his outstretched hand—and then made a futile grab for the photos, which slipped and spilled all over the floor.

"Oh, dear." She knelt to retrieve her photos. Jack Ferris did the same, and their knees bumped. Her head was inches from his chin, and she caught a whiff of clean male scent. Frannie quickly moved away. She felt as if the air grew syrup thick and heavy, making it hard to breathe this close to him.

In a moment everything had been gathered up and Frannie couldn't avoid looking at him, on his knees on the carpet, face-to-face with her. Time froze as she met his gaze again. She didn't know how he did it, but he made her stomach positively quiver when he was so near.

But it wouldn't do to let him see he affected her. She suspected he was used to women falling at his feet and she had no intention of encouraging him.

Summoning a wry smile, she extended her hand again. "Thank you, Mr. Ferris. Let's try this again."

"Please, call me Jack." He took her hand, the warm strength in his surrounding her much smaller one, reminding her forcibly that she was female, soft and giving, and he was all hard, unyielding male power. He helped her to her feet, but didn't release her hand. She couldn't free herself without making an issue of it, so she nodded as he led her to the love seat and chairs arranged around a coffee table topped with glass in the corner next to the wide window. "Why don't we talk over here? I'm not big on formality."

He seated her on the love seat before taking a chair angled next to hers. "So. You need some advice on marketing your—" he consulted a note on the yellow pad in front of him "—your sewing business."

"My bridal gown design business," she corrected. "What I do is create handmade wedding gowns and help the brides select accessories to complement the dress. I also design dresses for other occasions, and once in a while I'm asked to restore someone's grandmother's gown that has been packed away in an attic for fifty years."

"Sorry." Jack Ferris looked amused. "I didn't mean to insult you. I have the greatest respect for someone who wields a needle. I'm stitch impaired—can't even sew on a button."

She had to laugh at the description. "A lot of people tell me similar things. It's really not hard to learn the basics."

He smiled slowly. "My hands are too big. And I may have great reflexes, but my fine-motor skills are lousy. Anyway—" his eyes bored into her with that single-minded intensity again "—how can I help you?"

"I'm not sure." When his eyebrows rose, she went on. "I only opened the shop last year. It's gone well, even better than I expected in Westminster, and I'm considering a little modest advertising to introduce me to the Baltimore area on a larger scale. So far my advertising has been mostly word-of-mouth."

"How did you get it off the ground when you opened?" He leaned forward, genuinely curious, and she remembered that marketing was what he did for a living.

"Well, I have this friend who's…very good at getting her own way." She couldn't help the grin that spread across her face. "Once she decided to introduce me to a few people, I was busy instantly. Those people told other people, and—you know how that works."

"It only works if you have a quality product," he said. "So you must be good. Where did you learn to sew—sorry, design." His grin was unrepentant and cocky, as if he knew he would be forgiven.

"I studied at a school in Philadelphia for two years before coming back home."

"You're originally from the Westminster area?"

"Not exactly. I moved to Butler County at the same time I started the shop. My family lives in Taneytown, just up the road." She took a deep breath. "The thing is, Mr.—Jack, I'm on a tight budget. I can't afford a huge ad campaign."

"I have clients with all kinds of different needs." When he smiled at her this time, she was prepared. She doubted he was talking strictly about business, either, from the amusement gleaming in his eyes. But she wasn't in the market for a playboy who flirted with every female in sight, no matter how attractive he was.

She didn't smile in return. "I'm scheduled for displays at several local bridal shows next spring. I was thinking of some kind of brochure or flyer that people could take away with them."

Jack nodded. "That's a good first step for increasing your customer base. You've certainly got the right market." Again, that smile that invited her to step into his world. "All those brides-to-be with money to burn and dresses to be drooled over."

"Most brides-to-be are very budget conscious." The harder he tried to get her to relax, the more tense she became. She'd run into men like him before. One, in particular, and now she knew why he made her feel so uptight.

Oliver had been charming, too. Correction: Oliver had been good at *using* charm. Just like Jack Ferris.

Jack's eyes had grown thoughtful and faraway as he pulled up a yellow legal pad and began to take notes. "That's a good place to start. With affordability." He paused, and he was back in the present with her. "Are your gowns affordable?"

She nodded. "For handmade items, my prices are reasonable. I've compared them to a few others."

"Good." He scribbled furiously. "Why don't you tell me what you want to get across in a brochure. What do you want them to learn when they read about your gowns?"

Once he entered his business mode, he really was very efficient, she mused later, gathering her things together and rising to leave. Unfortunately, the flirtatiousness reappeared as he held the door for her.

"I'll be in touch," he said in a low voice, winking at her.

"I'll look forward to seeing your ideas for the brochure," she replied. She was forced to take his hand for one final seal-the-deal shake. Just like the first time, his hand was big and warm, and somehow as intimate as that darned smile.

Frannie spotted the wildly waving hands the minute she entered the deli, and she wound her way toward the table where her two closest friends in Westminster were waiting. She noted with amusement that Jillian Kerr already had attracted a man, who was hovering over her like a fish about to take a tasty bite.

"Hi, Frannie." Deirdre Patten rose from her seat almost desperately to hug Frannie. Dee considered men only slightly less threatening than big snarling dogs. Even something as harmless as having one determinedly buzzing around Jill was enough to put her on edge.

"Sweetie." Jillian rose, too, and came around the table

to kiss her cheek. The man with her was forced to step back, and Jill cast him a cheery smile over her shoulder. "Okay, Bill, time for you to do a disappearing act. This is strictly a ladies' luncheon."

Frannie grinned at her as the guy departed. "You never cease to amaze me. Has there ever been a time when you didn't wrap every man you met around your finger?"

To her surprise, Jillian's cheerful, confident smile wavered for a moment. "Once," she said, and grimly added, "but never again."

There was an awkward silence for a moment. Frannie could see that Jill would reject any comfort or sympathy, so she strove for a light note. "You know, you and Jack Ferris would make a good pair."

"Puh-leez!" Jill held up her two index fingers in a playful sign of the cross, as if to ward off the idea. "I've met Jack. He'll still be flirting when he's ninety. He's a handsome hunk, all right, but definitely not for me—I like a man I can control."

Deirdre giggled. "Forget Jack, then. He's really, really bad on a leash." Then she turned to Frannie. "So you went to see him? What did he say about your idea for a brochure?"

"He was going to work up a rough draft and price it for me. He was supposed to get back to me the next day. But it's been over two weeks," Frannie said. She raised her eyebrows and looked at Deirdre. "He wasn't what I expected. He's not the kind of man I'd think you'd be comfortable around."

Dee shrugged. "Jack and I grew up on the same street. My brother played lacrosse with him. He was just another brother underfoot for years."

Jillian eyed Frannie. "So what did our Miss Brooks think of Ferris the Flirt? Does that man make you drool, or what?"

"I thought you weren't interested in him." She knew she was avoiding a direct answer.

"Just because I don't want to marry the man doesn't mean I can't appreciate the way he wears his jeans." Jillian winked at Dee. "So what did you think?" she said again.

"Like you said, he's a flirt." Frannie shook her head. "When he turns on the charm, a woman just wants to fall at his feet. Which I'm sure many of them do. Which I'm sure feeds his ego nicely."

"Did *you* fall at his feet?" Jill feigned shock. "I thought you were immune to flirtatious men."

"He's not like that," Dee protested. "Jack's a nice guy. I don't think he's the kind who carves a notch in his bedpost."

"But we need to find out," added Jill. She pointed at Frannie. "You're elected."

"I don't *think* so." Frannie laughed, then sobered. "Besides, I'm less than impressed with his tardy response. I'm not sure I'd want to use him, even if his prices are reasonable."

"That's not like Jack," Deirdre said. "I rarely see him anymore, but unless he's changed, he's very prompt, especially with business matters."

"Oh, well." Frannie dismissed the topic as the waitress approached to take their lunch order. "At this point all I want is to get my portfolio of photos back. I need it to show to potential clients."

Two hours later she was staring in openmouthed shock at Jack Ferris's estimate for a brochure, which had arrived in her afternoon mail. And Dee said his rates were *reasonable?* Since Deirdre also had her own small business, Frannie had assumed she was as frugal as Frannie herself. Maybe she was. But one thing she knew was that it was going to be a while before Brooks' Bridals could afford to advertise.

Quite a while.

It was a disappointing thought. She'd been pleased—no, more like ecstatic—at the success she'd had since opening her business. Coming to a city, even a small one like Westminster, alone had been terrifying for a girl who'd lived with a large family all of her life. It had been strange not having anyone to take care of at first, so she'd thrown herself into her work.

And it certainly had paid off. She'd hired her first assistant seamstress recently, and four months ago she had brought in a part-time coordinator who went to the weddings and fussed over the last-minute details of making brides appear perfect. But it looked like she'd have to wait awhile before she grew any more. Especially if these were the current rates of advertising.

She went to the telephone and looked up the number for Your Ad Goes Here, Jack Ferris's company. The same girl who'd greeted her the day she'd been at his office answered the phone, and when Frannie asked for Jack, explained that he was out of town and was expected home soon. Frannie had to settle for leaving a message.

Five days later, she tried again. This time a canned message played and recorded her call. The same message was on the machine every day for the rest of that week, saying little except that the agency was temporarily closed due to a family emergency.

By the following Friday, Frannie was out of patience with Jack Ferris and his appalling business manners, family problems or not. This time she looked up his home number and tried it.

No answer, just his machine.

Doggone it, enough was enough. She'd been patient, and relatively pleasant, for a month now. This was inexcusable.

She needed those photos. If Jack Ferris wouldn't answer his phone, she was going to camp on his doorstep until she got back her portfolio.

The address turned out to be a pretty brick condo that looked spacious and pricey from the outside. She rang the bell five times, but no one answered, and she heard no voices or noise from inside. As she expected, the door was locked. Darn that man! In addition to being an annoying flirt, he was irresponsible. She'd told him during their meeting that she couldn't be without the photos for very long. He'd promised to call her within the week.

One week. Hah! Soon it would be four of them. She'd noticed a framed university diploma on his wall, so she knew he'd been taught to count. Obviously the lesson hadn't stuck.

The condo was an end unit. Anger made her bold and she marched around to the back and mounted the two-level wooden deck. There was a sliding glass door just to the left of an enormous barbecue grill, and she walked over and peered inside. The vertical blinds were pulled back, and she could see a kitchen with a dining area and beyond that, the beginnings of a living room. The counters were nearly immaculate, spoiled only by a lone coffee cup resting on its side and a newspaper which had spilled from the counter to the floor.

Weird. The place was immaculate otherwise. Those two small hints at sloppiness didn't fit. None of her brothers could manage to pick up after themselves, but it wasn't selective. Everything they owned was a jumbled mess. Maybe Jack had a cleaning lady who just hadn't been in yet this week.

Still...something bothered her. It looked almost as if Jack had gone tearing off somewhere in a tremendous hurry, and hadn't been back since.

Well, it was none of her concern, she told herself firmly, as she descended the wooden steps and walked back the way she had come. All she wanted was her property back. Then he could—

A silver sports car pulled into the driveway beside her van just as she opened the driver's door. Through its windshield, she caught a glimpse of Jack Ferris's face, which was obscured by the frame as the car slid to a smooth stop beside her.

Finally! She was elated. It was rare for her to get angry,

and rarer still for her to utter so much as a sharp word, but several choice ones sprang to the front of her mind. She started to step around to the driver's side, but stopped in her tracks, staring through the passenger side window. In the passenger seat was strapped an infant car seat.

And in the car seat was what appeared to be a very young baby, screaming its little head off.

Before the sight really had time to register, Jack popped out of the car exactly like a child's jack-in-the-box, arms waving wildly and hair disheveled. Only no one pushed him back down into his box. He sprinted around the car, sparing Frannie a distracted, mildly puzzled glance and a "Hi," as he tore open the passenger door and started to release the restraints holding the infant in place.

With the door open, the baby's shrieks increased in volume immediately. Its little voice sounded hoarse, like it had been screaming for a while, and its little fists and face were red with rage.

Jack scooped up the baby awkwardly, holding it loosely in one arm. His other hand made patting motions in the air near the child's kicking, cycling legs, as if he wasn't quite sure how to go about comforting the baby. Then he turned to face Frannie.

"Uh, Miss Brooks, right?"

"Yes." She strove to keep her voice crisp and professional, though it was getting more and more difficult to ignore the infant squalling between them. "I've been trying to contact you. I need my portfolio back. Immediately."

Jack juggled the child into his other arm and reached behind the seat for a pale yellow diaper bag, stuffed to the brim. The child kept screaming. "Oh, man..." He shook his head. "I completely forgot you. I bet you'd like to clobber me."

He straightened up and for the first time she saw how very weary he looked. His eyes were dull and red rimmed, and his hair was standing on end where it was long enough on the top. The squirming child slipped a little in his grip and Frannie reacted automatically, placing her hands beneath the baby's tiny body. She couldn't stand that screaming another minute. It cut at her soft heart and reminded her of all the nieces and nephews she'd rocked to sleep over the years.

"May I?" She slipped one hand up under the little wobbly head as Jack nodded immediately.

"Please," he said, and it was heartfelt. He released the baby and Frannie automatically shifted it into a close embrace against her shoulder, cupping the padded bottom with one hand while the other rubbed small, soothing circles around the infant's tiny back. She realized she had started a patter of gentle baby talk, rocking gently from side to side the moment the child settled into her arms, and she huffed out a breath of amused resignation at herself. Old habits came back dangerously easily.

Jack had gone around to the trunk and was lifting out a portable crib and several other bags. Buried beneath all the items he was balancing in his grip, he came around to Frannie's side and peered down at the baby. The child finally was quieting, its little chest catching in occasional spasms as its sobs subsided.

"How'd you do that?" he demanded. "She's been screaming since the moment we got off the plane."

Frannie was astonished. "You've been flying with her?" She realized the child was a girl as she noted his use of the feminine pronoun.

He nodded. "It's a long story. But I'm sure you're not interested." He hesitated. "Could you hold her until I get the stuff out of the car and set up this crib?"

Frannie nodded.

"The thing is," he said over his shoulder as he started for the door, "your pictures are at my office. If you can wait until tomorrow, I'll get my secretary to deliver them personally first thing in the morning. The office has been closed—that's why you couldn't reach anyone." He shook his head. "I'm really sorry. I thought I had all the loose ends tied up."

She trailed along behind him, crooning to the baby. Her portfolio seemed less important now, and she was ashamed of her anger. Whatever he'd been doing, Jack clearly hadn't simply neglected to get her things back to her. "That would be fine."

Stepping through the door, she took in the expensive furniture and the lush, deep pile of the carpet. Jack had dumped a pile of baby accessories on the couch and was pulling open the portable crib. Unfortunately, it was designed like most things that were advertised as easy to set up and take down. As fast as he pushed one side into place, another snapped back up. He finally got smart and planted one enormous loafer at one end, using his upper body to stretch the two opposing sides. That left one more side to be pulled into place, and Frannie took pity on him. She walked over and got a firm grip on the rail with her free hand. "Okay, now pull," she said.

The crib popped open and Jack stood back with a sigh. "Thanks. Why don't you just put her down in there while I get the rest of the stuff? She'll probably play or something until I get unpacked."

He was kidding. She hoped. Cautiously she pointed to a mechanism on the bottom of the crib. "You need to push this down to lock it into place. Otherwise, it could fold up with her in it."

Jack stared at the little lever. "Oh." He reached down and secured it. "It's a good thing you're here."

"Um, I hate to be a busybody, but I don't think she's going to be very happy if I put her down." Frannie glanced at the baby, who wasn't screaming anymore, but was definitely beginning to root around, banging her little head against Frannie's sweater in a vain quest for dinner.

Jack looked dubious. "Well, I'll take her. I guess I can unpack with one hand."

He started to reach for the child with a distinctly apprehensive expression on his face.

"Jack."

"What?" He paused.

She waited, but he seemed genuinely oblivious to the infant's increasingly restless behavior. Finally she said, "I think she's hungry."

He smacked himself in the forehead. "Of course! Why didn't I think of that? The lady on the plane said she'd probably get hungry every three or four hours."

This was getting stranger and stranger. Frannie couldn't imagine what Jack Ferris was doing with this baby. Clearly, he didn't have the faintest notion of how to care for her. "How long has it been since she was changed?" she asked.

He speared one hand through his hair and Frannie realized why it was standing on end. "I don't know. I guess since…I think one of the flight attendants changed her."

"You think? Where is her mother, Jack?" And why on God's green earth would she entrust her to your care!

Jack's shoulders sagged. "Her mother is dead." He looked at the baby. "I'm all she's got now."

Her mother is dead. Whatever answer she'd imagined, that one had been far, far from even making the list. Slowly, she sank down on the edge of the sofa. The weight of the baby in her arms suddenly seemed vitally warm and alive, precious and fragile. She looked down at the little girl, noting the dusting of blond hair, the flushed cheek and tiny, perfect lips.

"Do you mean you're keeping her?" She hated to keep asking intrusive questions, but her conscience would not, absolutely could not, let her walk away from this place until she was sure the infant was being properly cared for.

Jack sat down opposite her on a wide hassock. "Yes. I'm her legal guardian, and her only living relative." His elbows rested on his knees, and his big hands dangled between them. He dropped his head.

This puzzle didn't have enough pieces for her to even

frame it up with all the straight edges. "Is she...are you the father?"

Jack's head shot up. "Of course not!" He glared at her.

She shrugged. "It was a logical question." The baby was growing angry again, and she stood and rocked her. "Maybe we'd better change her and feed her."

"Right." He stood, too, and looked around for the diaper bag. Then he hesitated, turning back to her. "Miss Brooks—"

"Frannie." She smiled. "Miss Brooks is too formal for someone who's about to get spit up on."

"You'll stay for a while?" His face lit up so pathetically she would have laughed if the whole situation wasn't so sad. "I don't want to intrude if you have plans, but I need a crash course in baby care. Just the basics, until I can take her to a doctor and figure out this whole deal."

She wanted to tell him "the basics" were a major part of a young baby's life, but she sensed he was about at the end of his rope. "Sure. I can stay for a while."

He was a very different man from the self-confident flirt she'd met in his office last month. While she changed the baby—whose name, Jack said, was Alexa—he brought in the rest of the things he'd stashed in the car. Then he hovered, uncertainty radiating from him like a bad sunburn, watching her mix formula, test the temperature of the liquid on her wrist and settle down on the sofa to feed Alexa.

She realized he'd gotten a yellow legal pad at some point. "Are you going to try to work tonight? Because you really need to understand that babies—"

"I'm not working." Wearily, he plopped down beside her. "I'm taking notes on everything you did so I don't forget it when I'm on my own."

"There are books that can tell you this stuff," she said gently.

He'd let his head drop back against the couch and the notes lay half-finished on his lap. "How did you learn so much about babies?"

"I have three younger brothers," she said. "And two of them have children that I've helped to raise."

His eyes were closed and she risked staring for a moment, taking in the details of his profile, the enormous hands spread over thighs that looked heavily muscled even when disguised by his khaki pants. His jaw was heavy with stubble several shades darker than his hair, as if he hadn't shaved in a few days. It only emphasized how very masculine he was, as if she wasn't already aware of that.

As she shifted the baby to her shoulder to burp her, her arm brushed against his. It was like brushing concrete. No, that was wrong. Concrete didn't exude heat; concrete didn't tempt her to touch. His arms were as toasty as if he had a furnace inside, packed in solid muscle.

He turned toward her then, and she forgot all about her speculations. He was closer than their limited acquaintance dictated, and as he put one hand against Alexa's back, he leaned even closer. "Thank you," he said, and she watched his lips form the words with a fascinated detachment. How would those lips feel against hers? Would his kisses be tentative, persuasive? Or was he as sure of his kissing as he was of his flirting? If so, he would be a very dangerous man.

And this was a dangerous line of thinking. One she had no intention of pursuing.

"You realize a child is going to change your life completely," she said to him. "Are you sure there's no one more—no one else to take her?"

"I'm sure," he said. Although he still was turned toward her, his eyes were looking into a memory she couldn't share, and the sudden grief in his face unnerved her.

Without thinking, she put her free hand to the side of his cheek.

Immediately he covered it with his own, closing his eyes as if to savor the contact. "Alexa is my niece," he said. He released the pressure holding her hand in place, but turned his own and carried hers to his lap, where he played absently with her fingers. "My brother and his wife were killed in an accident."

Frannie could see the naked sense of loss on his face. "So your brother is—was her father?" It took a determined effort of will to ignore the gentle rub of his fingers over her knuckles.

"Yeah. Randy and Gloria had been trying for a long time to start a family. They were pretty thrilled when Alexa was born." He squeezed his eyes closed, as if to deny reality. "A tractor-trailer jackknifed and slid into them on a highway two weeks after she was born. Alexa wasn't injured because her car seat sat so low in the back seat—the whole top half of the car was sheared off."

Frannie stifled a small cry. Cold prickles of goose bumps spread down her arms and she shivered involuntarily. She turned her palm up and linked her fingers through his, gripping tightly. "Oh, Jack, I am so sorry. What a terrible tragedy." The full impact of the story sank in on her as the baby on her shoulder made a funny little lip-smacking sound and she realized this child would never know her mother or father, that her uncle Jack was the only family she had.

He sighed heavily. "I've been stuck in Florida for almost a month, disposing of their estate and straightening out the custody arrangements for Alexa." The small messy details of the coffee and newspaper she'd glimpsed in his kitchen through the back door made sense now. Those would have been the last things on his mind when he got that phone call.

Well, Alexa certainly could have fared worse. "She's a lucky little girl," she said. "I don't know a lot of men who would willingly take on a twenty-year commitment without some serious reservations."

"Oh, I have reservations," Jack assured her. "You've seen the extent of my child-rearing skills. Alexa might not think she's so lucky after a couple of days with me." A trace of humor surfaced in his eyes and then he grinned.

"And I don't know the first thing about how to handle puberty and dating."

Frannie's opinion of Jack Ferris had risen significantly in the past hour; now it rose even more. "I was thinking more along the lines of how a baby is going to torpedo your social life. Not to mention your romantic interests."

"Yeah, I can foresee some serious changes in my future. I may have to get married just to get some help with this." He indicated the child, now dozing on Frannie's shoulder.

He might have been joking, but his words struck a nerve she thought had been buried. "Why?" Her voice was crisp, reflecting the resentment that gripped her. "Women aren't automatically programmed to be the family caretakers."

"That's not what I meant."

"I have to be going." With the ease of experience, she shifted the sleeping baby into Jack's arms and set the bottle down on the coffee table. "I don't think she'll eat any more right now. She's exhausted. You'd better put her down and get some sleep yourself. She'll be hungry again in a few hours."

"Frannie, wait."

But she didn't want to hear any more. Whether or not he'd meant it, she couldn't pretend to be amused by his comment. Not when she had a vivid image of herself almost having been stuck in a loveless marriage solely for that very reason. "Relax. You'll be fine. You wrote down everything you need to survive tonight. Tomorrow you should call the pediatrician's office. They can recommend some parenting classes and books to help you."

She stood and looked around for her purse, telling herself she had no reason to feel guilty. This baby wasn't her problem. She barely knew Jack and she certainly wasn't responsible for helping him with Alexa. He would do just fine.

TWO

True to Jack's word, Frannie's portfolio was delivered to her first thing Monday morning by the same friendly blonde she'd seen in his office.

"I am really sorry about this," the woman said. "Jack and I had to coordinate a number of things by phone when he got called down to Florida, and I overlooked it."

"That's all right. Unavoidable things happen sometimes." Frannie hadn't been able to continue being piqued at Jack. Not after she'd lain awake half the night thinking about how he was doing with the baby.

"Jack tells me you were a godsend on Friday evening." The blonde smiled sympathetically. "I've never thought of Jack as a father in all the years we've been together. He certainly has his hands full."

The woman's words caught Frannie off guard. The way he'd flirted, charmed her last night had made her forget what kind of man he was. Anger lit a small fuse inside her.

He had no business flirting with her like that when he clearly had a long-term relationship with his secretary.

"It was no big deal," she said, practically shooing the blonde out and preparing to close the door. "I'd have done the same for anybody."

The rest of the morning she was conscious of a feeling of...disappointment nagging at her. It must be human nature to want to assume the best of someone. She'd given Jack the benefit of the doubt when she should have known better. Especially when she'd had first-hand experience with the same kind of man before.

Well, she wasn't going to give Jack Ferris another thought. She immediately called two clients and set up appointments for them to go over the portfolio with her, then went to work on a beautiful old dress that one client's mother had worn. The girl wanted to wear it, but unfortunately she was a bit larger than her mother. Frannie had devised twin panels of additional fabric as an insert at the waist that inconspicuously offered the necessary size adjustment. Both the bride and her mother were delighted.

In the middle of the morning, a delivery from the florist interrupted a final fitting for a girl whose wedding was the following Saturday.

"Got something here for you, Frannie," the man called.

Rising from her knees, where she'd been fiddling with the hemline that the bride insisted had be to lengthened to accommodate the higher heels she had bought over the weekend, Frannie pushed through the swinging saloon-style doors from the fitting area.

Her regular delivery man stood in the middle of the shop, totally hidden behind a huge spray of red roses beautifully displayed with ferns and baby's breath. His big feet in heavy work boots looked ridiculously out of place on the pale pink carpet. "You musta really impressed some fella."

"I can't imagine how," Frannie replied. "They're probably for one of my brides, though why they would have been sent here is a mystery."

"I don't know 'bout that," he said. He set the arrangement down on top of a glass counter displaying a variety of ladies' dress gloves. "It's got your name right here." He pointed to the address attached to the flowers before turning to leave. "You have a nice day now."

"You, too," Frannie said absently as she slid the small white card from its accompanying envelope.

You're my angel. Jack.

Pleasure swept through her. An image of Jack's face rose for an instant before the damper of reality intruded. Jack only was expressing his thanks with this too-extravagant gesture. He might have made her heart beat faster for a few hours, but that was immaterial. He was involved already. With at least one woman, she thought, remembering the phone conversation he'd been having the day she'd been shown into his office.

"Whoo-hoo! What did you have to do for those?" April, her assistant, peeked through the doors, then walked over to read the card as she bent toward the roses and inhaled deeply. "Who's Jack? And how come florists' roses never have any smell?"

"A little favor, a business acquaintance, and I don't know." Under April's suspicious gaze, Frannie fought the urge to fidget. It was true; Jack was just an acquaintance whom she'd helped out. The roses meant nothing to him other than, "Thank you."

And, of course, that was what they meant to her, too.

The rest of the week passed in a frantic blur. June was a big month in the bridal business; come July, the bell over the shop door probably wouldn't ring once the whole day, but it certainly was getting a workout in June. On Friday afternoon Frannie and April were sharing a soda and nursing fingers sore from so much detailed handwork, when the door to the shop's entry jangled yet again.

Wearily Frannie got to her feet. She would give a lot to be able to flip that sign over to Closed for the rest of the day. But they had fittings scheduled right up until they locked up that evening. With a sigh, she pushed through the doors into the shop with a smile firmly pinned in place.

She stopped dead when she saw Jack Ferris lounging against a counter, smiling at her. He was wearing a sort of backpack with Alexa snuggled into it, except that it was carried on his broad chest rather than his back. One hand patted a gentle rhythm against the spot where Alexa's back was. It was hard to tear her gaze from the sight. The contrast between the baby's pink, lace-edged bonnet and his big, blunt-fingered hand struck her hard in the heart.

He was wearing dun-colored slacks with a dark green knit shirt that made his eyes look silver. Or maybe it was just the light in the shop. Whatever, he looked wonderful. Her heart skipped a beat and her breath backed up in her throat for a minute. She despised her reaction, but she couldn't control it.

"This is a surprise," she finally managed. To her everlasting relief, her voice sounded relatively normal, if a bit higher than usual.

Jack straightened and came toward her, moving around the counter to her side. "I know. We just came from the doctor's office and I thought you might want to hear how Lex is doing."

"Lex?" To cover her flustered state, she seized on the name as she sidled a step away. "You're calling that beautiful little girl *Lex?*"

"Sure. Every kid needs a nickname." He took a step closer and smiled down at her. "Frannie is a nickname, isn't it? Short for Francesca?"

"Don't I wish." She shook her head as she backed up another step. "Short for Frances."

"I'm glad you're not Frances or Fran. I like 'Frannie,'" Jack pronounced, advancing again.

She didn't care what he liked. She just wished the man would quit invading her personal space. She took another step backward, and the wall brought her up short. "I like 'Frannie,' too." *Why are you here?*

"And Jack, of course, is another name for John. My father was John, and I have to say I'm glad. Don't you think Jack suits me?" He took another step closer.

"Jack suits you." She took a deep breath. "You're crowding me."

"I know."

She was startled into looking up and as she did so, she realized how very close he was. Their bodies were only inches apart, separated by the small mound of the baby's carrier. He was smiling that intimate smile again, and she reminded herself that it was second nature for him, that there was nothing personal about it.

"Do you do this to all your friends?" She made her voice light and amused.

At the outer edges of his eyes, the grooves deepened. "Only my absolute favorites." But he moved back a step.

She stayed where she was, with her back to the wall. Had she imagined it, or had his eyes grown watchful? "Thank you for the roses. It really wasn't necessary, though."

"I didn't do it because I thought it was necessary," he said. "I appreciate the time you took helping me with Alexa. She'd been in foster care practically until the moment we stepped on the plane. I've never been around babies much. It was a shock to have this little scrap of life dependent on me for every need all of a sudden."

"A first baby is a shock even when you've anticipated its arrival for months."

"No kidding." His voice was dry, and for the first time she noticed that he looked tired. "When people talk about how sweet babies are, they never tell you that they get you up in the middle of the night or that they throw up on you ten times a day and scream bloody murder when you give them a bath."

To cover her urge to laugh, Frannie coughed.

Jack's eyes narrowed. "That didn't fool me. You think this is funny, don't you?"

"Yes, but only because I've lived through it."

Jack cocked his head to one side, and his eyes suddenly were clear and alert. "You told me you helped with your brothers' children."

"Yes. Between them I have five nieces and nephews. One of my brothers' wives had twins a few years ago. They were premature and needed a lot of care for the first few months after they were released from the hospital." She smiled, remembering how fussy Robert's twins had been. "For about three months there, I was in desperate need of a few hours of unbroken sleep."

Jack was nodding. "It's only been a week, and I already feel that way. I'm keeping my fingers crossed, though. For the past two nights she's slept for five hours straight. I think we're on the right track."

Alexa stirred and he looked down. "What's the matter, baby doll? Are you tired of being crammed into that sack?" He glanced at Frannie. "Would you like to hold her?"

She really shouldn't. She was up to her eyeballs in work. But she could already feel the sweet weight of the little body in her arms. "I'd love to."

He lifted Alexa from her nest and passed her into Frannie's hands, and she noted that in just one week he had gotten pretty sure of himself. It showed in the careful, competent way he handled the child as he untied the bonnet's strings and lifted the little cap from her head.

"Hello, sweetie. How's my girl today? I bet you're having fun with your uncle Jack." She used the special voice she reserved for teeny ones as she clucked and murmured.

Jack chuckled. "I don't know if we're having *fun,* but we're managing."

Alexa yawned and grimaced, and her blue eyes focused intently on Frannie's. Then her tiny face crinkled in a wide grin.

Could a person's heart melt? Frannie felt as if her whole being suddenly had softened as a rush of maternal delight swept over her. "Oh, look! She's smiling at me."

"She'll smile at anything right now."

"Thanks a lot. That was flattering."

"I guess that didn't come out quite right." He chuckled again. "One of my clients brought her a rag doll that's almost the size she is. I set it in the corner of the crib and every time she catches sight of its face, she smiles."

Frannie rocked the baby as Alexa stretched and cooed. "You know a friendly face when you see one, don't you, chickadee?" Holding Alexa up, she brushed her cheek across the down-covered scalp, then lifted her head to smile at Jack. "This has got to be my favorite age. I adore them when they're tiny and helpless and they look at you like you're God. Then again, toddlers are delightful, too. Just in a different way. And they're really fun when they hit school age...."

Her voice trailed away. He was still standing too close, but she'd forgotten when she'd been absorbed in the baby. Now she remembered.

He was looking at her mouth as she spoke. It was a silly thing, but it struck her as unbelievably seductive. Even when she stopped speaking, he didn't meet her eyes, but continued to watch her lips.

Time stopped. Her breath stopped. Deep in her abdomen, she felt a flower of warmth blossoming, unsettling her, the excitement of arousal stirring and softening her in a manner totally different from the maternal feelings she had for Alexa.

Slowly he lifted one big hand, up and up and up until it was hovering at her cheek. His index finger feathered a whisper of sensation along the bow of her upper lip; his gaze followed the motion.

She kept her own eyes on his face, studying its blunt contours, the broad sweep of his brow, the sandy lashes that formed a thick screen about his eyes. Had she ever seen a man so beautifully formed before?

Jack lifted his gaze to hers. Time stretched and sagged around them while he silently seduced her; in the depths of those bottomless silvery eyes she read a multitude of messages. All of them conveyed arousal, and a desire that curled her toes inside the comfortable flats she was wearing.

Alexa chose that moment to utter a full, resounding belch worthy of the bowling alley or the golf course.

Frannie jumped and looked down at Alexa.

Jack's gaze flew to the baby, too. Slowly that heart-stopping smile spread over his face as he looked back at Frannie. "Wow. If she were a man, I'd consider that a challenge."

Frannie laughed, feeling the tension of the last few moments shatter as she handed the baby back to him. "Here. You'd better take her. I seem to have an adverse effect on her."

"Hardly." Jack's voice dropped to a lower pitch. "You've had a great effect on her. And on me."

Butterflies rose in a flurry of sensation in her stomach. Doggone it. He was the worst flirt she'd ever met. Mentally she kicked herself for succumbing to his charm, if only for a moment, and willed herself to ignore the mad beating of butterfly wings. "Well, thanks for stopping by. It was nice to see you both. I hope the adjustment period continues to go as smoothly."

In the act of resettling Alexa in her little sack, Jack paused. "Um, Frannie?"

For a moment she'd swear a look of...almost guilt, she supposed, crossed his face. Then it was gone, and he was affable, incredibly attractive Jack again. "I really have to get back to work now," she told him.

"I know. This will only take a minute. I have something I'd like you to think about."

Think? He wanted her to think? I think seeing you again, even in a chance meeting, is a really bad idea, she told him silently. He could make her forget too much, offer too much—

"I need to find someone to baby-sit for Alexa while I work. Would you consider keeping her?"

"Would I...?" It took a moment to sink in. Frost swept through her, and the butterflies died in the chill, becoming a dead weight in her stomach. Outrage rose. There was little she disliked more than men who used their charm to wheedle women into doing them "a favor." She felt like she'd hopped onto a carousel horse that kept bringing her around to the same old point again and again. Did she have a sign stamped on her forehead that read Nursemaid or Housekeeper?

It was a struggle to keep her expression blank. "Who's keeping her now?" she asked carefully. Beneath the surface, anger began to consume her, boiling higher and higher every second.

"I've been taking her to work with me," he said. "Between Marlene and me—she's my secretary—we've been managing, but it's just too hectic. She really needs to be with someone who has more time for her."

"So what makes you think I have the time?"

There was a bite in her voice now, and Jack looked cautious, as if he'd wandered into the middle of a minefield and was trying desperately to pick his way out intact. He looked around and spread his hands to indicate her shop. "I just—this is attached to your home, isn't it? You sew, which doesn't require dealing with people constantly, and you're fantastic with her—I know you love children."

She dug both hands into her hair to keep from putting them around his thick neck. "Yes, Jack, this is attached to my home. Do you know why? Because during the big bridal season, I'm too busy to even take time to drive to work and back." Her voice rose. "And just how do you suppose I make clothing that *fits* my clients?"

"I don't—"

"I have people wandering in and out of here all day long for fittings and design sessions and fabric consultations. I have customers scheduled right up until eight o'clock tonight. Come here."

She turned and marched to the back of the shop and

pushed through the doors into the fitting and sewing room, seeing it through Jack's eyes as he followed her.

A three-way mirror with a platform in front for viewing clothing was mounted at one end of the room. One wall was filled with shelving on which were sewing supplies, dozens of different fabrics, bridal magazines and accessories. Hats, veils, shoes, hosiery, frilly white parasols and clever little beaded purses filled shelves to overflow. The wall opposite the mirror was one enormous closet. When the doors were folded back as they were now, more than fifty dresses in various stages of completion could be seen hanging. Against the fourth wall were three sewing machines. Directly behind them was an enormous, custom-designed worktable on which April was pinning a pattern to a swath of satin. Two ironing boards stood beside it. Everything was neat and tidy, but it was clear this was a busy place to be.

"Does this look like I have time to baby-sit?" she demanded, turning back to Jack.

Behind her, April said, "Hi, I'm April. Are you Roses-Jack?"

"That's me," he said. "It's nice to meet you, April. Do me a favor and tell the coroner I died from having large quantities of roses stuffed down my throat."

April laughed, clearly delighted, and Frannie thought bitterly that he could get most women to do just about anything. Too bad for him, she wasn't most women. Anymore.

"April, take a break. Go drink a soda, take a walk, go in the house and watch a soap opera," Frannie told her.

April's eyes rounded. "Yes, ma'am." She laid down her shears and exited the workroom through Frannie's private door.

"Look, Frannie, I'm sorry," Jack said.

"No, you're not." Her voice was hard. "You might be sorry you weren't able to sweet-talk me into keeping your baby, but you're not sorry you tried to con me into the job. Do you realize how shallow you seem? You've spent your whole life using your charm to get women to do your bidding, haven't you? I bet ninety percent of your clientele is female, because they're easier for you to manipulate than other men.''

"You'd lose the bet." His voice was as chilly as hers was heated.

"You never expected me to refuse, did you? You just assumed that because I loved your baby—and yes, I admit I'm wild about children—I'd be happy to help you out once you batted your eyes at me and smiled.'' She held open one of the doors leading to the shop out front. "Too bad for you I've met charmers before. As a breed, you're distinctly unimpressive. Now, if you'll leave, I have work to do.''

Jack's face was grim. He hesitated for a moment, and Frannie was shaken by the black fire in his eyes. "Then I'll leave you to it.''

He moved toward the door, and again she was struck by how graceful he was for a big man. As he reached her, she stepped back so he could pass, but he paused, forcing her to look up to meet his eye. And even though she knew he was deliberately using his size to intimidate her, she quailed inwardly. She only hoped it didn't show, and she lifted her chin higher in defiance.

"You're wrong about me, but you were right about one thing. I'm not sorry I tried to con you into keeping Alexa. My biggest concern is finding someone who will love her as much as I do. I knew she'd be safe—and loved—with you.''

He turned and brushed through the doors, and her whole body sagged as the angry electricity in the air went with him.

She absolutely could not *stand* him. She should be pleased with herself that she had stood up to him. Instead, his final words echoed in her ears, making her feel small and mean—and guilty.

The rat. He probably knew exactly what he was saying, and how it would affect her.

The match was tied, 3 to 3. As he sprinted down the lacrosse field, one eye on the lacrosse ball, Jack caught his attention wandering away from the game. It wandered toward the same place it had about every thirty seconds throughout the match—toward the bleachers off to the right, where Frannie Brooks had sashayed her little butt up onto a bench right before the game began.

He'd been so shaken up when he first saw her that the coach had to call his name three times to get his attention. What in tarnation was she doing at his match? He was positive he'd never seen her here before. For about ten minutes, he'd entertained the fantasy that she'd sought him out, that she had come to apologize for the things she'd said almost two weeks ago—eleven days, if anybody was counting.

Which he wasn't. The opinion of one girl with wide, serious eyes, the most kissable mouth he'd ever seen and incredibly sexy legs didn't matter one whit to him.

After a few minutes of watching her, while waiting for the match to begin, he realized that she was with the sister of one of his teammates, Dee Halleran—no, she was married now. Or at least she had been. Her brother had said she was divorced.

Just then, Dee said something to Frannie as she turned and pointed straight at him. Frannie looked at him, too, and he saw the shock in her face. There was no way she had known he would be here, he could tell, and she apparently hadn't recognized him beneath his face mask. Dee waved, but he pretended he didn't see her as the coach gathered the players for last-minute strategy. It must be simple chance that Dee had invited her to come along. He knew they were acquainted because Dee had been the one to refer Frannie to him.

Just then, another attackman passed off to him. He

caught the pass easily with his stick and barely had time to send it hurtling toward the goal before the center from the opposing team came at him with bared teeth and narrowed eyes, slamming him hard in the chest and knocking him to the ground.

A scream went up from the sidelines. His teammates were dancing around—ridiculous behavior for a bunch of big guys in face masks—and one man extended a hand to help him off the ground. "Way to go, buddy!" He pounded Jack on the back.

Jack winced. He was getting too darn old for this sport. He'd said that every year for the past five, but this year he meant it. Next season, the only way he'd be stepping onto a lacrosse field was as a coach.

Turning toward the bench, he gathered his stuff into his oversize duffel. Now where the heck was the woman who was watching Lex? She'd reluctantly agreed to keep Alexa during the matches so that he could finish the season, and he knew why. She was as competitive as her husband. If Jack didn't play and the lineup changed at this late date, it would shake everybody's confidence. And that would be a bad thing right before the championships.

He spotted the woman's blond hair at the far end of the bleachers. Shouldering his duffel, he headed her way.

"Hey, there," the sitter said as he approached. "I think your kid needs to be changed."

She held Alexa out and plopped her into his arms, then slipped the diaper bag over his shoulder atop the duffel as he peered down at the baby, who appeared to be sleeping peacefully. Though she did indeed smell as if a diaper switch was in order.

"What's the matter, honey?" Her husband came up behind her, turning her into his arms and kissing her. "Does that baby make you nervous?"

"You know it." She laughed. "It's going to be a few more years before I'm ready for the kind of commitment a baby takes."

He smiled down at her in an intimate manner that Jack envied. "I think we need a few more years to practice, anyway, just to be sure we're going about making babies the right way."

They had their arms around each other's waists as they walked away. It was easy to admit he envied them. He'd wanted that kind of closeness once, and for a while he thought he had it. A short while.

But he didn't want to go down memory lane tonight. What he wanted was to talk to Frannie Brooks. Actually, he'd almost be content with the view, he thought, assessing her legs exposed by the shorts she wore. He stopped beside Deirdre, who was talking to her brother.

As he smiled at the two women before him, he was feeling a little jumpy around the edges. Much as he hated to admit it, he owed Frannie an apology. He'd been planning to call her, but this was better.

"Hi, Jack." Deirdre greeted him with a warm smile, her heart-shaped face lighting up. She looked...worn down. Not just tired from too little sleep, but wiped out, as if she was running on nerves, having depleted her reserves of energy. Surveying her two little boys, who were racing up and down the field with a couple of sticks they'd sneaked off with when the owners weren't looking, he could see why. Those two would keep anybody on the edge of insanity.

"Hi, Dee." Wrapping his free arm about her shoulders, he gave her a gentle peck on the cheek. "How are you?" It wasn't a routine courtesy; he was concerned. He'd known her since they were kids, and he knew things hadn't turned out well between her and the jerk she had married. She hadn't been to a game all season, which was unusual in itself.

"Passable." She brushed off his query and indicated the woman standing silently to one side. "You've met Frannie, I believe."

"Hello, Jack." Her voice was quiet but not as frigid as

he'd expected. Or as frigid as he deserved, maybe. She had been right to be ticked off by his assumption that she could fit a baby into her schedule more easily than he could. He couldn't figure how he'd come to that idiotic conclusion; fatigue was his only defense. He'd been so wiped out after dealing with the estate and taking on Alexa his brain cells were making faulty connections.

"Hi, Frannie." He should apologize, but his tongue was stuck to the roof of his mouth. Her little nose was so straight he thought he might have to run a finger down it just for fun, and her eyes were as flirty as ever above the lush curve of her lips, though he was pretty sure she didn't know how she looked. She was wearing shorts of blue jeans material, with a pretty checked shirt that didn't quite meet the waistband of the shorts. With each move she made, he caught a tantalizing glimpse of smooth, bare midriff. For some reason, even though her clothing wasn't painted on or skimpy, she reminded him of a comic strip he'd read as a kid in which a hillbilly girl thoroughly filled out the briefest imaginable clothes. He'd always liked that comic strip.

"How's Alexa doing?"

Her voice startled him. Good thing she wasn't a mind reader. As he tried to catch her eye, he noticed that she looked at the baby rather than at him.

"Pretty well," he said, forcing his mind to make rational conversation. "She has her first cold, but we're scraping along pretty well together."

"Lee! You may not hit your brother with that stick!" Deirdre looked over her shoulder at them as she trotted toward her sons, who were now tearing into each other with the sticks. "I'll be back in a minute, Frannie, and then we'll go."

The silence was uncomfortable after she left.

He cleared his throat. Hurry up, Ferris, eat all the humble pie in one big bite. "Look, I'm sorry about the other week. I was a jerk and I don't blame you for being mad—"

"Hey, Jack! Give me a call." One of the "groupies"

who followed the team patted him familiarly on the butt as she walked by.

He wanted to snarl at the woman to keep her hands to herself and tell her she'd grow old waiting for him to call, but as usual, the manners his father had drilled into him kicked in, and he gave the girl a wave and a smile. "Hey, Iris."

When he looked back at Frannie, she had a blank, polite expression on her face. "Apology accepted," she said briskly. But in her eyes, he could see an "I told you so," and he knew she was marking another tally of condemnation in the column labeled Reasons to Write Off Jack.

She started to turn away, but he grabbed her arm, holding her in place. *Great, Ferris, really smooth. Real polite, grabbing her like some ape in a zoo.* He suddenly felt stung by the same emotion he'd felt the day she'd practically kicked him out of her store. It wasn't anger, and it wasn't annoyance. And it couldn't be hurt, because he'd have to care about her for her to hurt him. But her classification of him as a...a playboy who didn't care about women had really pushed his buttons.

He'd thought about the encounter every day since then, examining his conscience for twinges of guilt that might identify her accusations as fact. Fact was that he liked seeing women smile, liked knowing he'd made them feel good for a few minutes in their day. Fact was that he never was rude intentionally to the fairer sex, even when they annoyed the hell out of him. Fact was that he honestly didn't go around seducing women every place he stopped. And fact was that while he'd had his share of liaisons over the years, he wasn't indiscriminate, and the number wasn't in double digits, as she clearly believed.

"You're really wrong about this," he said. "I'm not some kind of superman with women."

"I never said you were," she pointed out.

"Look," he said. "I hate being at odds with people, and

I don't feel like you're happy with me, even though you theoretically accepted my apology.''

"There was nothing theoretical about it.''

"Yes, there was.''

"I told you I accepted your apology.'' She glared at him.

He knew she was serious. He wanted to be, but it was just too much. Her little chin stuck up in the air as if she were daring him to throw a punch, and her eyes were stormy. Her brown hair was straight and shiny. It framed her face and he found himself fascinated by her lips, as he'd been every time he'd seen her. She looked as kissable as any girl he'd ever met.

"You're going to accuse me of flirting if I say this, but I swear I'm not. You just look...really, really cute when you're mad.''

"I'm not mad!''

The charged silence lasted for a long moment. Then, as he raised one eyebrow, her face melted into amusement and she laughed ruefully. "Okay, so I was mad. I'm not now.''

"Good. Friends?'' He knew as he held out his hand to shake hers that he was going to have more than friendship from her one day, that he was going to have her in his bed for a long, long time, until whatever magic she worked on him faded and friendship was all that was left. But it probably wasn't wise to explain that to her right now.

"Friends,'' Frannie said.

The diaper bag chose that moment to slide off his shoulder, and Jack juggled Alexa, the bag, his duffel and his stick while he hitched the strap back into place.

She put up a hand to help him, and her fingers slipped briefly over his. *Pow.* There it was again, that explosion of awareness. He was aware of her in a way he'd never been of a woman before, and when he touched her skin...his own skin did some very interesting things.

When she'd come into his office that first time, he'd noticed she was attractive in a quiet way. He'd been trying to get off the phone from...he forgot the name, but it was a woman he had no plans to call. Ever. And he wished she'd quit calling him.

Frannie had perched sedately on a chair and a bit of leg slipped out from beneath her slim skirt, and his interest had picked up. He had decided to ask her out for dinner if her personality was as nice as her package.

And then she'd dropped those papers and they'd knelt together on the floor picking them up. She'd paused and looked into his face—and the strongest rush of physical need he'd ever experienced hit him like a solid blow from an opponent. For two cents, he'd have taken her right there on the floor. He'd been so astonished he'd just stared at her until he realized he must be making her uncomfortable. He'd never had such a difficult time keeping a meeting on a business footing.

She, on the other hand, had been cool and collected, interested only in what he might come up with to promote her business. She'd walked out of his office and he'd decided to hurry and get the business transaction out of the way so that he could ask her out.

And then he'd gotten a phone call from Florida that changed his life and chased every rational thought out of his head.

What was it about her that hit him in the gut every time she was near? She wasn't curvy or top-heavy like most of the girls he'd dated, though her legs were nicely trim and her ankles slender. Nor was she blond, another common denominator in his past preferences. She was just… incredibly sexy. Arousing. All of his senses perked up when she got close; his body forgot he was a civilized man. He could almost smell her, although he couldn't have described it.

Alexa was waking up and he looked down at the baby. His baby. He was beginning to appreciate just how much his life was going to change. He couldn't ask a woman out right now—what would he do with Alexa? He still hadn't been able to bring himself to leave her with a sitter. She came to work with him each day, although it was getting more and more difficult as she grew and changed every week.

"Somebody's getting hungry again," he said to Frannie.

"Babies tend to do that." She smiled. Then she hesitated. "Jack, I've been meaning to call you."

Great!

"I'm not going to be able to use your ideas for the brochure right now. The one you came up with would be lovely, but I just can't swing it right now."

Deirdre, sons in tow, was advancing across the grass toward them. He couldn't think. As Alexa began to voice a protest at having to wait so long for a dry bottom and a bottle, Frannie reached out and stroked a finger over one tiny hand before she turned away. "I'll see you around, I'm sure."

Three

Alexa had been extraordinarily fussy all day.

Jack paced around the condo with her in his arms as her screams got louder and angrier. What was he doing wrong? He'd checked the usual cause of unhappiness—wet diaper—and tried a bottle, but she'd refused it. She hadn't slept in hours.

Neither had he, for that matter. It was almost midnight on Saturday night.

His anxiety mounted. He thought she seemed hot, so he took off her little sleeper. Maybe that would make her happier.

But she shrieked louder than ever. He paced around the table in his dining area so many times he was sure he'd worn a path. God, what could be wrong? He knew next to nothing about babies before Alexa. Now he knew almost next to nothing.

He wished he had Frannie's expertise and years of experience. He'd bet Frannie would have Lex happy and gurgling in her usual good-natured way if she were here.

The thought barely registered in his brain before he knew what he was going to do.

He fumbled the phone book out of the drawer, found her number and punched buttons with his thumb.

One ring. Two rings. Oh, no, he'd forgotten it was the middle of the night. She was probably sleeping.

Or out on a date.

"Hello?"

He'd never felt a rush of relief so sweet. He didn't know whether it was because he needed help or because he knew she wasn't out with some other guy, and he didn't much care. "Frannie? Hi, it's me. Jack. I'm really sorry about the time. I forgot it was so late, but the thing is—"

"What on earth is wrong with that baby?" Her voice sounded alarmed.

"I don't know," he said, speaking loudly to be heard over the screaming. "I've tried everything I can think of. I thought maybe you could suggest something."

"Do you want me to come over?"

"Please. That would be great. If it's not too much of an imposi—"

"I'll be there in ten minutes."

On her end, the phone clicked off abruptly.

His knees felt weak and he sat down before he fell down. Lex was still screaming bloody murder, but now he could handle it. Frannie was coming.

Her van whipped into his driveway exactly eight minutes later. He knew because he was counting. How many traffic laws had she broken? Didn't matter. He'd gladly pay every ticket she incurred.

"Let me look at her." That was all the greeting she offered. He surrendered his screaming niece to another pair of arms and waited expectantly.

Frannie had barely touched Lex's little body when she

raised her head, and the look on her face scared him to death.

"What is it?"

"She's burning up with fever. Jack, call your doctor right now. I'm going to put her in a cool bath and sponge her down until you talk to him."

He scrambled for the phone again, listening as Frannie carried the screaming baby up to the bathroom. It occurred to him that she would need towels, but as the doctor's answering service came on the line, he decided Frannie would find anything she needed.

Twenty minutes later they were on their way to the hospital.

The nurses in the emergency room steered Frannie to an exam room the minute they walked in. Frannie didn't even hesitate as she carried the infant down the hall. A doctor walked toward him, explaining that he had spoken with Jack's doctor and that he'd be examining Alexa.

He nodded. He was dying to be back there with them, but first he had to stop at the desk and give them his insurance information.

As soon as possible, he joined Frannie in the exam room. She stood against a wall, arms folded tightly over her chest, as a doctor and nurse bent over Alexa, who was shrieking and screaming on the table. Without speaking, he slipped an arm around her shoulders. Just that simple action was comforting. He didn't feel so alone, or so terrified.

They had a diagnosis in under ten minutes. Alexa had whopping infections in both ears.

He felt like the lowest of the low as the doctor handed him a prescription. "We've given her a little medication to bring that fever down and knock out the pain. Once that takes effect and I'm satisfied the fever's on its way out, you can take her home. Right now, you could go and have this filled. There's an all-night pharmacy right across the street. Your wife can stay with the little one."

He caught Frannie's startled glance out of the corner of

his eye, but he didn't even bother to correct the guy. If she really was his wife, they probably wouldn't be here right now. She would have known Lex's personality change wasn't sheer contrariness, but a sign of illness. She would know about diaper rash and when to start solids, about shot schedules and growth curves and developmental delays...all the stuff he'd been reading about in the few spare moments he'd had since he became Alexa's father by default.

If he were to marry again, not that he was considering the idea, Frannie would be the type of woman he'd choose, he thought as he waited for the pharmacist to fill the prescription. She loved Alexa, and she knew stuff about raising kids that he'd never even heard of. Their sex life would be fantastic. At the mere thought, his body went on full alert— and he did mean full alert, he thought ruefully, so that he had to turn hastily and examine the display of literature on the wall near the pharmacy. If he wasn't careful, the lady pharmacist was liable to have him arrested as some kind of pervert who got off reading medical pamphlets.

So enough about what it would be like to sleep with Frannie every night. Even the idea of falling asleep with her snuggled close against him was appealing.

Forget it. Wanting to be close was what got you in trouble the last time, dope. Why would you want to set yourself up to get shot down again?

The answer was simple: he wouldn't.

With prescription in hand, he jogged back across the street and into the emergency department. Seeing him, the girl at the desk smiled warmly and stood. "I think they're ready to go." She disappeared, and in a few minutes Frannie came out through the swinging doors from the E.R.'s interior, carrying Alexa.

He held up the bag to show Frannie he'd gotten the medicine, suddenly feeling incredibly weary. Alexa wasn't screaming anymore, but the sound of her pained cry would haunt him for a long time. Why in the world hadn't he realized she was hurting? It didn't take a rocket scientist to be a parent, even a half-decent one. Which, no doubt, was what Frannie would say.

The little receptionist who'd greeted him a moment ago held the door open for Frannie. She beamed again, dimples flashing in her rosy cheeks when she saw Jack. "I hear this little one isn't your daughter. She's so *precious*. And you're so lucky to have a wonderful friend to call on." The girl advanced on him as Frannie started for the door. "Here's a card with the number of the hospital to keep by your phone in case you need help again. And my number is on the back. If there's *anything* I can do, just give me a call. I'd be happy to help anytime."

Jack took the card she extended without even glancing at it. "Thanks very much. I'll keep that in mind." The girl gave him one more toothy, cheerleader smile as he held the door for Frannie.

He eyed Frannie's back as he strode after her. When he reached her side, he slowed to match her pace. "I know what you're thinking. That *wasn't* my fault. Did you see me making eyes at that girl?" Frustration colored his voice, and he forced himself to take a deep breath. He had the feeling that she would sprint in the opposite direction if he tried to make her understand he didn't even *want* to look at another woman these days. Finding he still held the white card in his hand, he methodically ripped it into tiny shreds and dumped it into a trash can they passed.

Frannie turned and looked at him, and to his amazement, she was laughing. "You do *not* know what I was thinking."

"Ha."

"Really," she insisted. "I was thinking that I can't imagine being as forward as that woman. She homed right in on you, buddy."

"Too bad," he muttered. He didn't see one thing amusing in the incident.

"You need sleep," she told him. "I've never seen you grumpy before." As they reached the car, she waited until he opened the door for her to strap Lex into her seat, then opened the front door for Frannie. As she stepped into the car, she looked up into his face and he saw she was still laughing. "It's kind of cute."

Cute? She thought he was cute? He chewed that one over as they drove back to his condo. It wasn't a very manly word; he probably should be offended. But it was the first sign she'd given him that she didn't find him completely objectionable, and instead of growling some more, he felt a bubble of satisfaction growing inside him.

Frannie watched Jack warily as he unlocked the condo door and ushered her inside. He was looking awfully smug about something. He made her nervous when he got that look on his face. She'd already learned it meant he was hatching some idea.

To cover it, she said, "I think you'll be able to get her to sleep after she has a bottle. She must be exhausted. You're supposed to start her on the antibiotic immediately but keep giving her pain reliever for about twenty-four more hours."

Alarm flared in his eyes. "What if she starts to cry again? Couldn't you stay until she's asleep?"

She glanced at her watch. "Jack, it's one-thirty in the morning. I have a busy day tomorrow. I have to get some sleep."

"You're working on Saturday?"

"Until the end of June and the mad rush to the altar subsides, I work every day."

He grimaced. "I'm really sorry for calling you. I didn't stop to think."

She stifled a yawn. "It's okay."

"Why don't you stay here?"

It surprised her, and she knew it showed. "Stay here?"

"It makes sense. You can get some sleep, but if Lex and

I need help, you'll be here." He took her hand in his free one, and his eyes were earnest when he gazed down at her. "Please, Frannie. You can have my bed and I'll take the couch." Then he grinned, and the Jack she knew was back again. "Unless, of course, you'd like to share the bed. That makes even better sense."

"Only to you." She forced the flippant words out. How was she supposed to refuse when he was looking at her like that? Even though she knew the man could talk a Frenchman into buying California wine, he got to her. And when he was this close, touching her, seducing her with his mere presence, she didn't have a chance.

"All right." If she agreed, then she could put a tiny bit of distance between them, at least. "But you're sleeping on the couch. You can pretend to be a gentleman."

"It's a deal." His broad chest expanded and fell again. The mere fact that he didn't parry her verbal jab told her a lot about his mental state. "Thank you. I'll never be able to thank you enough for all you did tonight." He didn't release her hand, but lifted it to his lips, and she felt the moist, sweet caress of his mouth against the back of her fingers. "Come on. I'll get you some fresh towels."

It was a good thing, she decided, that he hadn't noticed the involuntary shiver that seized her at the contact. As she followed him up the steps to the second floor, she told herself it was just a physical thing. She hadn't had a date, hadn't been kissed by a man in so long that all it took was one little innocent gesture to get her heart pounding and put a funny, aching sensation deep in her abdomen.

He guided her toward the master bedroom at the far end of the hall. On the way, he pointed out a spare bedroom, which he used as a home office, and a third bedroom which had been turned into Alexa's room.

It didn't look like a room for a baby girl. Unadorned and bare, a crib, a changing table and a zillion boxes were its only decor. "I want to wallpaper it after I unpack all her things," he said with a sheepish grin, "but there don't seem to be enough hours in my days anymore."

"It won't get any easier." She looked at the child, dozing now in his arms. "The older she gets, the busier you'll be."

"Thanks for the encouragement." His tone was wry as he laid the baby gently in the crib, covering her with a pink blanket before moving toward the big bedroom that she knew was his. "Here's where you'll sleep." He switched on a light. "There are T-shirts in the top drawer of the dresser and an extra blanket in the closet."

She nodded, trying to act casual as the silence stretched. The enormous water bed that dominated the room seemed to magnify the fact that she was alone in a bedroom with Jack.

His eyes were on her, but suddenly she saw that they weren't actually seeing her. His eyes were glazed and he practically sweated dejection. He looked...really, really bad. Exhausted, certainly, but something more.

"Are you all right?" she asked.

He shrugged and shook his head like a dog coming out of water, then sat down on the edge of the bed. "I guess." He didn't sound convinced. Then he looked straight at her and his gaze was focused, intent. "Do you think I'm doing the right thing?"

"The right thing...?" Inviting her to sleep in his bed?

"Yeah. Do you think I should keep Alexa?"

The question staggered her. The direction of his thoughts began to coalesce in her head. "Of course you should keep Alexa. Didn't you tell me you are the only family she has left?"

He nodded.

"She needs you, Jack." Frannie perched beside him on the bed. "Family is important."

"I know. That's what I told myself when I applied for custody. But tonight...tonight showed me just how bad I am at this parenting stuff." He looked at her, and she read anguish and despair in his gray eyes, sorrow that made her want to pull his head to her breast and comfort him as she would a child. "She had a mother and father who loved her. They never thought they wouldn't live to see her grow up."

The sorrow in his voice reminded her that Alexa wasn't the only one who'd lost someone dear to them. Jack's brother had died. She didn't know what to say, so she followed her instincts. Turning to him, she put her hands as far around his wide shoulders as they would go and pulled him to her. It was an awkward embrace; he was so much bigger than she. But he was still in need of comfort and she certainly knew how to offer that.

"Do you know what I'd give to bring them back? For her sake?" His voice was muffled against her hair. "I'd give my own life for that baby girl in there to have her parents again."

"Sh-h-h." She stroked the back of his neck, feeling the warmth of skin give way to the soft stubble of his short hair under her hand. "It doesn't work like that. You can't trade one life for another, as much as you might wish you could. You just have to move on from here, think of how lucky Alexa is to have you."

"Lucky? I damn near killed the kid tonight. I don't know anything about raising children."

"That's an exaggeration." She made her voice firm and authoritative, sensing that was what he needed right now. "So you didn't realize she had an infection. Yes, she was sick and uncomfortable, but she wasn't dying. And you've learned something from the experience. Now you know how to check for fever and what to do if she is hot. You know how to administer medication and you have some sense of when to call the doctor. You're not going to kill her, Jack. You're learning something every day. I was surprised at how easily you handled her the day you came to see me. If you'd seen yourself that first day..." She chuckled a little at the memory. "Let's just say you made me a little nervous."

He drew back far enough to gauge the expression on her face. "I guess I've gotten a little better with her."

"A little? Could you have changed a diaper a month ago? Mixed formula? Would you know which end to hold upright to burp?"

"Okay, I get the point." She was relieved to see his eyes clearing. "I couldn't have done any of those things without you, though."

"Sure you could have. You might have learned them a little more slowly, but you'd have figured it out."

"I'm glad I didn't have to." His deep voice was fervent. Then his tone changed. "Tell me about your family. Are your brothers older or younger than you?"

"All younger." She slipped her hands down from where they still rested on his shoulders, aware of every warm inch of him only millimeters away. The position was far too intimate for friends who didn't even know each other that well. "My mother died when I was twelve, and I helped my dad take care of the boys after that."

"A surrogate mother." He captured her hands when she would have drawn away.

"I suppose." His thigh was warm and solid where it pressed against hers, his fingers big yet gentle. She was afraid her voice would show him how breathless she felt.

"How old were your brothers when your mother died?"

She thought for a moment, forcing her awareness away from the sensual promise in his proximity. "Eight, five and the baby had just turned two."

She felt his interest quicken, honing in on her with an unsettling laser accuracy. "Holy smokes. That's a big burden for a young girl."

"I guess it is. You don't think about that when something happens to your world."

"I know." His voice was dry. "So what did your father

do when you graduated from high school? Did you go away to school?''

This wasn't a period of her life she particularly enjoyed rehashing. She felt the weight of those years settle on her as if it were yesterday. "I was supposed to go to a clothing design school in Philadelphia. My dad had a heart attack in July the year I graduated from high school. He survived, but there was no way I could leave him alone to care for all three boys. I thought I'd wait until they were all a little older. But then he died the following spring and I became my brothers' legal guardian."

"So you delayed going to school again?"

She nodded, her throat suddenly too knotted with regret for words to come out.

Jack's eyes were steady on hers, and suddenly the room was too small, too intimate. The air around them seemed to shrink inward, sealing them in a bubble in which nothing existed except intense, wordless communication. She didn't know how it had happened, but her world had been cut apart recently, and when it was patched, Jack was stitched into the fabric of her days.

She thought of him too often. Too many times his face floated between her and the work she should be focused on. Too many times she'd caught herself sitting idle, scissors or needle arrested in midair as she wondered how Jack and Alexa were doing.

His thumbs caressed her knuckles as his eyes dropped to her lips, lips that felt parched and dry. Without thinking, she licked them, and a flame leaped high in his eyes as his head came down, blotting out the light.

Alexa's fretful cry from the next room made her jump. Frannie asked herself what in the world she was doing? Frantically she turned her head.

Jack's lips landed on her cheek, and she was shaken to her toes by the sweet scrape of his stubbled jaw against her neck. She froze, and so did he. In the quiet room, she could hear her own breathing mingled with the heavier rasp of his. More than anything, she wanted to turn her face to his, to let him take her and do anything he wanted with her willing flesh.

But she knew better. Jack came with all kinds of complications. He might not be the playboy she'd taken him for initially, but he definitely was not what she needed in her life.

She bounced up with all the false enthusiasm of a cheerleader celebrating a tie-breaking touchdown and turned toward the door. "There's Alexa. It's time for more pain medication, and she'll probably be hungry. I'll—"

"I'll get her. You need to get to sleep." Jack's hands caught her at the waist as he stood, as well. He pulled her against him, and she gasped as his bold masculinity, solidly pressing into her belly, proclaimed his interest in her. His hard, lean frame was seared into her consciousness, and his hot breath feathered over her temple.

"Frannie."

"What?" Her voice was a strained whisper; she dared not look at him.

"We haven't finished this."

She surfaced slowly from a deep, dreamless sleep. No, it hadn't been dreamless. She'd been dreaming that she heard a baby crying.

But it wasn't a dream. It was real. As she remembered where she was, she realized the sound she heard was Alexa.

She threw back the light cover and left the bed. As she turned toward the door, the glowing digital display of the clock announced that it was four-thirty in the morning. Alexa wasn't screaming yet, just beginning to fuss. As soon as Frannie picked her up, she stopped, making little mewling sounds of relief.

"That's my baby. That's my girl." She rocked back and forth, rubbing the baby's back as she grew quiet, feeling the frantic squirming lessen. "It's no fun waking up all alone, is it?"

With deft hands, she laid the infant down and changed her diaper, picking her back up before Alexa could get wound up again. When she put the child against her shoulder, Alexa began butting her head against Frannie's collarbone. She recognized the signal—Alexa was programmed to search for sustenance. "Are you hungry? I know you didn't eat enough last night. Your poor ears were hurting too bad. Let's go find your uncle Jack."

The words gave her pause as she remembered the early-morning intimacy they'd shared, but she brushed the memory aside. It would be tomorrow in just a few hours and she'd be gone with the first light. Jack hadn't really meant those whispered words; he might have been aroused and determined at the time, but he'd think better of it in the morning.

Padding down the stairs with the child sucking furiously on her pacifier, she walked through the living room. Jack lay on the sofa, oblivious to their presence. He was on his stomach, with his face buried in one arm. The other trailed over the side of the couch and lay, relaxed and limp, on the carpet. The couch must have been purchased with his comfort in mind, she decided, because it was long enough to accommodate his whole length.

She couldn't bring herself to wake him, so she tiptoed into the kitchen. He had to be exhausted after his frantic worry over Alexa and their midnight hospital tour. Why wake him when she was already awake?

Quietly she mixed a bottle of formula and heated it, then carried both the baby and the bottle up the steps. There was no rocking chair, no place even to sit in Alexa's room, so she settled herself against a mound of pillows in Jack's bed and fed her there. By the time the bottle was empty and Alexa was asleep again, Frannie was fighting to keep her own eyelids from drifting shut. The baby's room seemed a long way down the hall, and they were both warm and comfortable... Scooting down, she laid the baby beside her and arranged pillows on the far side so Alexa couldn't accidentally fall off the bed. She'd just keep her right here so she could hear her before she woke Jack the next time....

She was awakened by a fly landing just below her ear, tickling. Still caught in the warm, drowsy state of half sleep, she waved her hand to brush it away.

When a big, warm hand engulfed hers, she jerked and her eyes flew open. Jack's face filled almost her entire field of vision as he lay propped on one elbow looking down at her.

She searched his dancing eyes for a moment. "What are you doing?"

He was sprawled across the other side of the bed, judging from the way the covers were pulled taut over her hips, and blind panic surged as she remembered the baby. "Where's Alexa? She was sleeping right here with me."

"She's fine. I moved her over between those two pillows. When I woke up a few minutes ago, I thought I'd check on her. She was sleeping like a little soldier right here with you cuddled around her."

Her body sagged as relief flowed through her. "I thought for a moment you might have laid on her, or she rolled off the bed—"

"You worry too much." He shifted closer. There was something she needed to say to him...but his free hand rested warm across her soft belly and his face hovered above hers... She was shocked at how desperately she wanted to know his mouth, wanted his kiss, needed it to soothe the aching tingle that made her hands tremble as she put her palms up to his naked chest and stroked over the furred planes, over his collarbones and out, to the smooth muscles of his shoulders and upper arms. It was a tacit gesture of acceptance; she was tired of fending him off when she really didn't want to, and he read it in her eyes. Slowly he lowered his head.

When his mouth covered hers, she nearly cried out in relief. For weeks now she'd wanted this, even if she hadn't been able to admit it to herself. As his arms gathered her

closer against him, she knew only that this had been between them, waiting impatiently to be acknowledged, since
their very first meeting. She moaned, and he responded by
smoothing his hand over her belly, sliding his palm surely
up over the T-shirt to cover her breast in an intimate claim
that, despite the thin layer of fabric that prevented true sensation, had her murmuring in delight and pressing closer
against him. He shifted his weight to lie half over her, easing one leg between hers, and her body sang.

"I could get used to this." His voice was husky and deep
as he broke away from the kiss with a deep intake of breath.
He nuzzled his way along her neck.

The words were an unwelcome intrusion into her easy,
lazy, sensual haze. She stiffened as she came more awake,
came more alert and realized that she was in Jack's bed,
with his weight sprawled across her and her arms around
his neck. She pulled her hands away from the heavy muscles she'd been gently tracing. "Stop."

Did he even hear her? "Jack, stop."

Slowly he drew back a fraction to inspect her face, which
probably looked as thoroughly kissed as she felt. He was
silent for a long moment, and she couldn't begin to guess
at his thoughts but the look on his face froze her in place,
temporarily shutting off her breath on a rush of caution.
His normally open, friendly expression had vanished. His
eyes were narrowed and intent; they glittered with silver
fire. A brush stroke of red color rode high across each
cheekbone, and he was breathing heavily.

She knew an instant of purely primal female vulnerability. He was all male at this moment, a taker, dominant and
commanding. If he chose to disregard her words, she knew
he could, without uttering a single word, finish the heated
lovemaking these caresses promised. A taut moment
passed. Then she felt his body relax where it was pressed
against hers, though he still didn't move.

His face relaxed, melted into the easygoing mask he
wore for most of the world. A facade she now recognized

hid an implacable will and a deep, fierce streak of determination.

"Sorry." There was a smile in his voice, though his eyes were still watchful. "I woke up and came looking for Alexa. The sight of you in my bed overwhelmed my common sense."

She snorted and pushed against his chest insistently, more sure of her ground now that he was teasing her again. The only way to get past this awkward moment was to joke. "Men are overwhelmed by my beauty all the time."

"I didn't say you were beautiful." He rolled off her to lie beside her again, propped on one elbow.

The words were a slap in the face, the hurt unexpected and deep slicing. The good humor that had accompanied her mixed emotions at release vanished abruptly. She shoved at him, struggling to get away, to leave the bed, but he caught her wrists and held them easily in one big hand. Then he moved over her again, using his superior strength, forcing her to stay where she was.

She turned her face away, using the only avenue of escape he left her, and her body stilled against his. He was the worst kind of cad she'd ever met, seducing women he wasn't even interested in. She'd die before she'd let him know how his kisses had aroused a huge, throbbing need in her, how even now her body was urging her to move beneath the hard demand of his.

"You didn't let me finish that thought," he said, and his words were hot puffs of molten air against her cheek.

She wouldn't listen, wouldn't even give him the satisfaction of indicating that she knew he'd spoken.

When he bent and set his lips against the pulse that beat in the side of her neck, her body jolted. She squirmed and shrugged to deny him access to the sensitive spot, but he only transferred his heated kisses to her jaw. He made an appreciative hum low in his throat and she realized he was enjoying her movements. "I didn't say you were beautiful," he said against her skin, "because that's the wrong word to describe you."

"Spare me your astute observations." Turning her head, she glared at him.

"Don't be obtuse." For the first time she heard a hard edge in his tone, and when he raised his head, his eyes were pewter, dark and stormy, as he glared right back.

Ha! She knew it. Underneath that velvet glove was an iron fist. But what did he mean, telling her not to be—

"You're a very desirable woman. You waltzed into my office in that prim little business suit, and all I could think about was how fast I could get your clothes off. A man senses softness beneath your surface and he wants it for himself. Beauty is a shallow word." He paused, and his face relaxed into less rigid lines. "There's nothing shallow about you."

She swallowed, searching his eyes for truth. If this was a line, he was even slicker than she had given him credit for. If it wasn't...

Why did he have to be so darned sweet? He was much easier to fend off when he was doing his macho male impression. She could feel herself yielding, losing the anger that had strengthened her resolve to resist him. "I have to get going," she mumbled, looking away and avoiding his eyes as she pressed against his shoulders with her palms. "I have a lot of orders I want to work on today."

"Okay." In one lithe move, he was off the bed. He lifted her in his arms and then let her slowly slide down over his body until she was on her feet. Then, while she was still too shocked and aroused to even think of protesting, he took her by the shoulders, pulling her to him and sealing his mouth on hers in a deep kiss that immediately blazed into a hot, uncontrollable exchange of passion.

Her head fell back and her arms came up; she was moldable, malleable clay in his grip for one long second until suddenly he tore himself away. His chest was heaving, but his eyes were dancing with pleased complacency as he said, "Think about that while you work."

He walked around the end of the bed and lifted Alexa from the nest of pillows, then strode from the room without looking back.

She dressed in the clothes she'd thrown on when he called last night, washed her face and decided not to bother with what little makeup she had in her purse, and did the best she could with her hair. Then she slowly went down the steps.

Jack was sitting in the living room feeding Alexa a bottle. The sight of the big man with the tiny infant in his arms did something funny to her middle, as it did every time. He looked up, smiling, as she hovered by the stairs. "You're welcome to have breakfast before you go. I don't have much, but there's cereal and fruit."

"No, thank you." She hesitated. "Jack, I'm sorry for—that I didn't—"

"I'm sorry that you didn't, too." His grin was rueful, but then it vanished and he regarded her with sober eyes. "Frannie...I like being with you. Not just because you've helped with Alexa. Not just because if you crooked your finger, we'd be in bed faster than you could say please. It's a combination of a lot of things. But I have to be honest with you. I'm not looking for a relationship. At least, not for anything beyond friendship and a great time in bed." He shrugged, and looked out the window. "It sounds bad, I know. But that's all I have to give. And if you aren't interested in more than the friendship part, that's okay. I'd like to be your friend."

"I'd like to be your friend, too." Her voice was low. "But right now I don't need the complications that anything else would create."

"I can live with that." His easygoing smile was back in place.

She was beginning to hate that expression. He slipped that mask on as if he'd had years of practice. Even his display of temper last night had been more honest, more real, than this. Where was the real Jack Ferris?

Crossing to his side, she regarded the baby slurping down her breakfast. "I'd like to stay in touch. I'm starting to feel like I have a vested interest in this little one's future."

"She's going to need people who love her," he said. "How about if I call you in a few days. We can go out for a meal or I could cook, depending on how Little Miss is scheduled at the time. Just friends." But there was a glint in his eye that made her swallow and be glad he had his arms full of baby.

She took a deep breath and the words poured out, even as she told herself she was doing something incredibly stupid. "That would be nice. But as a friend, how about if you come to my place and I cook? You have your hands full already. Is Thursday night good for you?"

He nodded. "Thursday night would be great."

Four

Jack swiveled his desk chair around to stare out the window at the shimmering waves of heat distorting the concrete landscape of the street outside. The early-summer sun was baking everything in sight. Baltimore was caught in the throes of a heat wave.

Sort of like me, he thought. Tonight he and Alexa were going to have dinner at Frannie's house. He'd thought of little else all week.

He really should respect her wishes. But a part of him, the part that could lie without compunction and promise without conscience, knew that no way were he and Frannie destined to be "just friends." No, unless nuclear war ended the world in the meantime, he was going to get her in his bed.

The mere thought had him gritting his teeth and taking a deep breath as the fit of his dress pants suddenly changed radically. He'd been plagued by these unexpected, sudden hard-ons all week, ever since she'd lain beneath him in his bed. It was like being fifteen again, one big out-of-control hormone fest. He'd hated it then and he hated it now. No, he hated it worse now. A grown man should have more self-control.

But he was afraid that word didn't exist in his body's reaction to Frannie Brooks. How could she ignore the desire that ricocheted between them?

He knew she felt it, that he wasn't the only one affected. He'd seen her breath grow shallow and her lips get dry. He'd watched the taut tips of her nipples rise beneath her soft cotton shirt and he'd felt the hot, sweet response of her mouth under his for far too short a time. She gave off a searing heat that damn near melted him every time he got close.

Well, the only melting he planned to do was directly connected to a slow, satisfying rise in the horizontal temperature he and Frannie created.

But he wouldn't push her. He could almost see the struggle going on inside her when he'd told her he wanted her. And it wasn't only connected to the physical thing. She seemed completely unaware of what a challenge she presented to men. Or maybe she wasn't unaware so much as she was deliberately discounting her effect. She gave the impression of being wary, of evaluating any compliment and refusing to allow it to warm her.

Her mental evasion aroused every hunting instinct in his masculine cells. He'd figure out why she was so elusive. When he had her beneath him, her legs climbing his back and her hips begging him for release, he wanted more than simply physical pleasure.

He wanted all of her.

He wanted her. No one else, just Frannie.

It was hard to face, wanting a particular woman again, and he made himself say it again. He'd sworn he was done with relationships. He'd spent five years in a marriage with a woman he'd been sexually infatuated with at first. Once that had worn off, he'd discovered that he didn't know the real woman very well. And the more he got to know, the less he liked.

Lannette had used sex to get what she wanted. And he'd liked her flirty ways. At first. Later, after they'd been married, he'd noticed she still didn't hesitate to turn on the charm with other men. She'd been very used to getting her own way. When sex didn't work, she'd used tears. Immature. That's what she'd been. It was probably a good thing they'd never had kids, even though he could still feel the sting of rejection he'd known when she'd told him she never wanted children.

And yet, despite his resolve, here he was, practically forcing himself into another relationship with a woman who didn't seem at all sure she was interested in him the way he was in her. But there'd been moments...the night she'd helped him when Alexa had been sick, for one. Yes, Frannie was wary. But uninterested? Not after that kiss.

He shifted uncomfortably in the leather chair again, grimacing as he put down a hand and adjusted his unruly body, and it occurred to him that sitting around thinking about Frannie was masochistic. Reluctantly he swung back to his desk and glanced over the file for the last appointment of the day.

Then he heard Alexa. Uh-oh. He glanced at his watch. Man, that kid could eat. He headed for the bassinet he'd bought and set up in the corner of his office. When he'd started bringing Lex to work, he'd sort of counted on his secretary to do the motherly thing. What he hadn't counted on was her aversion to anything that smelled like sour milk, spit-up or dirty diapers most of the day.

"Jack, you and I have worked together for a decade. Have you ever heard me cooing over babies or talk about becoming a mother?" She'd looked as panicked as he'd felt the first time the social worker had dumped Lex into his arms. "It might be a natural instinct for some women, but I'm definitely going to have to learn it. And I'm not ready to start practicing yet."

So much for help from that corner.

Once he'd gotten the hang of handling a baby, it hadn't gone too badly. But Lex was growing visibly every week, and as she did, she was beginning to stay awake for longer and longer periods of time.

As he slung the diaper bag over his shoulder and headed out to the car with Alexa, he realized that he was going to have to bite the bullet and hire a baby-sitter, even if the person didn't get a perfect score on his mental list. None of the places he'd investigated seemed suitable. He'd seen horror stories of infants mistreated by supposedly loving caregivers, and he was terrified by the thought of Alexa in the hands of some maniacal nanny five days a week. She was his baby now, and he was going to do this parent thing right.

Randy and Gloria had loved the little scrap of life with every fiber of their beings; he'd heard it in Randy's voice when he'd called to share the news of Alexa's birth. He, Jack, could do no less. He still got choked up when he thought about his brother and his wife. One week, they'd been celebrating Alexa Dianne Ferris's birth. The next, they were dead and Lex was an orphan.

Sometimes life really sucked.

He was still chewing on the baby-sitter problem when he arrived at Frannie's house an hour later. As he stood on the doorstep, he decided to widen his search—

The door swung open and Frannie appeared before him. "Hi."

She was wearing casual clothing, a denim skirt short enough to show him those legs he spent way too much time dreaming of. With it, she'd paired a snug-fitting short-sleeved sweater that clung to her shoulders, blossomed over her breasts, nipped in at her waist and lovingly settled over the beginning curves of her slender hips. He'd die a happy man if he were that lucky sweater.

"Hi," he said, forcing himself to converse like a normal human being. Which he knew he was because his body was telling him so in no uncertain terms. It was going to be a long evening.

She had prepared chicken shish kabobs, which were just about the best thing he'd ever tasted. Marinated, she explained, to give them flavor. She asked him a question about his business and they spent most of the meal discussing various forms of advertising.

Afterward, she rose and began to clear the table. Lex was happy for the moment in her seat, so he helped, scraping plates and loading the dishwasher while she washed pots and pans.

"You're pretty good at this," she observed.

"Necessity. I've lived alone for a long time."

"I haven't." She paused reflectively, then shrugged her shoulders. "It's certainly much easier to keep the house clean, but I miss the sounds of other people. Do you know what I mean?"

He nodded. "Yeah. I was used to it before, but if Lex wasn't there now, I'd think the place was a tomb. Speaking of whom—" He glanced over at the baby, waving her fists diligently in the infant seat. "I hate to eat and run, but I'd better get going. This is about the time she usually gets her bath."

"If you like, I could bathe her for you. I have some mild skin cleanser that would be safe." Her eyes were eager and he grinned.

"You just want to get your hands on my baby, don't you?"

She smiled back, holding up her arms in mock surrender. "I confess." As she lifted Lex out of the seat and cradled her in her arms, she said, "There is nothing in the world quite as wonderful as the feel and smell and sight of a baby."

He was still thinking about the blissful look on her face ten minutes later while he caught the news. She had insisted he relax for a few minutes, and truthfully, he was grateful.

In the kitchen, her telephone rang. She was in the bathroom with the baby, and he knew she couldn't hear it. Her machine could pick it up. After a ten-second debate with himself, he rose and went to answer it.

"Hello?"

"Who's this?" The male voice was clearly startled and less than happy.

"This is Jack Ferris. Who's this?"

"I must have a wrong number." The note in the man's tone became apologetic.

"If you're calling Frannie Brooks, you've got the right one. Can I tell her who's calling?"

"Where is she?" The guy really sounded disgruntled now, and apparently he had no intention of giving Jack his name.

Well, two could do this dance. "Frannie's got her hands full at the moment—" literally "—but I can take a message."

"No. I need to talk to her." The man didn't sound happy at all to find he had competition. Jack could sympathize— he hadn't known Frannie had another man in her life. But when it came right down to it, he didn't know very much at all about her. It was a state of affairs he intended to correct.

Frannie came down the stairs, carrying Alexa wrapped in a big towel. The infant was squawking; he knew she hated to be taken out of her bath. "Who is it?" She approached the phone and Jack switched receiver for child with her.

Jack shrugged. "A man. He wouldn't tell me his name." He found the pacifier, and Lex immediately lowered her volume to an occasional sucking sound as she gave the small item a good workout while he stuffed her into a sleep suit and brushed her shock of fine hair to one side.

"Hello?... Oh, hi, Robert...Jack's a friend and that's not your concern." Her voice was warm and affectionate, but he recognized a note of warning layered beneath. "So how are the twins? Tell them Aunt Frannie misses them."

Twins? Aunt Frannie? He suddenly felt a hundred pounds lighter. Not competition. A brother. That doesn't mean she doesn't have any other relationships, he cautioned himself. But he couldn't keep from grinning stupidly down at Lex, snuggled in his arms.

"Yes, you heard a baby." She didn't elaborate. "The twenty-ninth? I don't know. It's in the middle of the week. I'm not really sure I can get away. I'm already keeping all the kids for both of you guys on the seventh, remember?"

Another silence. This time, when she spoke, her voice was cool. "Robert, you know the answer to that. I'm just not available for baby-sitting now. My shop is doing better than I ever expected—I'm swamped with work... That's silly. The twins are old enough to get along quite well with another baby-sitter."

She listened again and laughed, although to his ear, the sound was a bit strained. "You're not talking me into it. Don't count on me for the twenty-ninth. I have to go. I love you. 'Bye."

He heard the little beep, which signaled she had disconnected practically before the farewell was out of her mouth.

"Brothers." She shook her head and set down the hand unit with a noticeable thump. He noticed she took a deep breath and exhaled slowly, as if she were making an effort to contain her temper. After a moment her shoulders relaxed and she came over to fold herself into a pretzel on the blanket where Alexa was bicycling in place.

He was stretched out on his side with his head propped on one hand, one ankle crossed over the other. He tried to sound casual as he asked, "Problems?" He sensed that this part of her life was a key to unwrapping her reserve, at least to a degree, and he was dying to know why she'd looked as if she wanted to take a bite out of her brother.

"Not really." She picked up a two-inch sock that had come off Alexa's foot and replaced it, wrestling with the vigorously moving little limbs. "The boys can't get used to the fact that I've actually started a successful business."

Then she glanced at him across the blanket, and the sweet smile she tossed his way wiped all coherent thought from his head, stirring the male longing he'd kept under wraps since she'd opened the door. "Robert shifted into interrogation mode when he heard you and Lex. I won't be surprised if he wants a copy of your medical records, your birth certificate and your rabies vaccination."

"Protective sort, is he?"

She laughed. "Any man I speak to is a candidate for marriage. The two older boys consider it their duty to keep an eye on me."

Marriage. Her words shocked him more than they should have. He was unsettled by the wave of possessiveness that rolled through him at the thought of her marrying some other man. "I take it they've tried to marry you off."

A shadow passed across her expression. "Unsuccessfully." Then she smiled. "I think they're afraid I'm going to be an old maid."

He grinned at her wry tone. "Hardly. How old are you?"

She looked startled. "That's not an acceptable question for a gentleman to ask a lady." She smiled, and a dimple flashed in her cheek. "But since I'm not sensitive about it...I'm thirty-two."

Now he was the one who was startled. He'd figured she was somewhere around twenty-five or twenty-six. Obviously she'd left out a few details in her life history. He did a little quick math. If she'd only started her business a year ago, and she'd gone to the standard four-year college, that meant she hadn't even started higher education until she was twenty-seven. What had happened to her twenties?

"I didn't mean to shock you speechless."

He recognized that slightly defensive look in her eyes. If he questioned her directly, she'd evade him. He made up his mind to ask Deirdre to spill everything she knew about Frannie the next time he saw her. "You didn't. I was just thinking that I wish I were thirty-two again, instead of thirty-five."

"Yes, thirty-five is so-o much older than thirty-two."

"Ha, ha." He reached over and tweaked her nose. "If I were thirty-two, I'd still have three more years to play lacrosse."

"You're quitting after this year?"

He grimaced. "I prefer the term, 'retiring.' I've been playing since I was a kid."

"If you still enjoy it, why are you qu—retiring?"

It was a hard question to answer, and his response was slow. He put his hand over Alexa's stomach, absently noting the contrast between his huge paw and her fragile baby bones. "Several reasons. First of all, it takes up too much of my time now that I have a child. I want to be there when she's awake, when she takes her first step, and starts jabbering away. Second, now that I have Lex I can't afford broken bones. Lacrosse is one of the roughest contact sports in the world." He shot her a rueful grin. "I want to get out while I'm still the one delivering the contact. And the third reason is that I'd have to find a baby-sitter several times a week for the whole season. Even longer if we go to the championships. I'm having a hard enough time finding someone to watch her during the day."

She was nodding. "Good reasons."

"Speaking of baby-sitting…relax. I'm not trying to talk you into anything."

She had drawn back and was frowning at him as if she expected him to ask her to keep Alexa again. At his final words she smiled. "Sorry."

He told her about his difficulty finding a day care setting he was happy with, about how many people he'd interviewed and how many places he'd visited. "Maybe it's me," he said finally. "Maybe I'm being too picky."

Frannie shook her head, and he was momentarily distracted by the silky fall of her dark hair sliding against her cheek. "You can't be too careful about your child care provider," she said. "If you feel uncomfortable with someone or someplace, trust your instincts. Women don't have a corner on intuition, you know."

"The trouble is that my instincts warn me about everybody."

She laughed. "There are some wonderful people out there. Keep looking."

"I'll have to. This can't happen fast enough."

"Taking her to your office isn't working?"

He felt his good spirits deflating. "That's an understatement. My office manager doesn't do babies."

Frannie licked her lips, and though he was certain she wasn't even aware she'd done it, the sight of that small pink tongue sent a serious surge of blood coursing through his body. He had to concentrate to remember what he was talking about.

"Lex seems to have a knack for fussing during my most important client meetings. I wish I could make it work, but I can see it's only going to get more and more difficult as she gets livelier."

Frannie nodded. "You're right about that."

Silence fell between them for a moment, then Frannie began talking to Alexa. Lex's little mouth worked, as if she were trying to mimic the motions, then her face crinkled into a wide, toothless grin and she squawked.

Frannie was delighted. "She smiled at me!" She was bent over the baby, and he swept his gaze over the graceful curve of her back. The urge to reach out and lay his hand along her spine was almost irresistible. To slide his palm beneath the short sweater and indulge himself in her soft, silky skin, to simply feel the life in her, warm and vital under his hand.

But he knew any such action would send her dancing backward ten paces in their relationship. To get his mind off her body, he blurted out the first thought that came to mind. "So why haven't you married? You're great with kids."

She straightened, slowly taking her hands away from the

baby, and the animation that had played across her face a moment ago went out like a birthday candle being extinguished with a single breath. "That's exactly why I haven't married," she said in a dull, quiet tone.

What did she mean by that cryptic comment? He was about to question her further when she rose and picked up their empty iced-tea glasses, carrying them to the kitchen, where he heard ice rattling into the sink, followed by the dishwasher opening and closing. A hint that the evening was over.

"Frannie?" He rose, too, and followed her. Meeting her in the doorway, he deliberately kept his tone light. "I didn't mean to ruin the party. Can we just erase that last question from the computer logs?"

She made an effort to smile, and he pretended he didn't see what an effort it was. "I'm sorry. You hit a nerve."

He forced a hearty laugh. "Sorry. I was just making conversation. Tell me about your brothers...if that's a safe topic."

"It's safe." She tucked her hair behind one ear. "What do you want to know?"

"What was it like, raising three little brothers? Didn't it cramp your style?"

She considered the question. "I didn't think so at the time because I didn't know anything different. Looking back, I'd have to say I probably missed out on a lot of the fun, silly things most teenage girls do." She shrugged and smiled, looking at Alexa. "I'd do it again the same way, though."

"I know you told me you didn't go to college right away, but what did you do with your brothers when you finally started school?"

"I didn't." Her tone was so flat it startled him.

This sounded like a conversation that was going to get intense, so he deliberately phrased an outrageous question to lighten the atmosphere. "So that framed diploma on the wall of your workroom is a lie?"

"Of course not!" Too late, she saw his smile. "I did go to school. Just not right away. And did you know that you're a terrible snoop?"

He grinned. "You just had to sneak that in there, didn't you?"

She pulled her face into exaggerated lines of mock seriousness. "I apologize profusely."

"I accept." He looked down at Lex, who had fallen asleep in his arms. "Looks like somebody winked out. I suppose I'd better get her home to her own little bed."

"Yes." She glanced at the clock over the sink. "I hate to have to throw you out, but it's getting late and I have a big day tomorrow."

"No problem. I am nothing if not flexible." He turned toward the living room and began gathering up the baby's items. "And you're right. It's getting late for us, too."

Ten minutes later he was out the door and heading for home, with Lex snoozing in her infant seat behind him. It had been an educational evening in more ways than one, he mused. He'd learned that Frannie was fiercely protective of her privacy, even with her family. And he knew there was a huge unexplained chunk of time that she hadn't mentioned in her past—a time when she was...doing what? He'd find that out another time, he promised himself, smiling a little. But the smile died half-born as he recalled the way the evening had ended. She was so good with Lex, and she seemed to enjoy her so much that he'd assumed she wanted kids of her own some day.

But it was looking pretty certain that liking them and wanting her own were two very different things in her head.

And, of course, that was fine with him. He enjoyed spending time with Frannie, but it wasn't like he was planning to marry her. Although it was true he had thought about marriage again since Lex had come along, it was still an amorphous cloud of half-formed ideas in his head. He sure wasn't taking applications yet. No, when he spoke wedding vows again, it would be solely to secure a good mother for Lex, perhaps someone who would give him a child or two of his own, a companion who had a life of her own that would mesh with his without demanding anything more than warm friendship and physical intimacy. Lannette had shown him how foolish it was to need a woman; he didn't have to be shown twice how stupid he'd been.

She'd done him a favor when she left, though he hadn't seen it that way at the time. He'd considered marriage to be a permanent state, and even though his had some serious cracks in its outwardly smooth surface, he'd have stayed married—miserable, but married—for the rest of his life. Lannette had taken that choice from him, and in doing so, had given him a second chance.

Somewhere out there was a woman who fit the requirements he'd realized were necessary in a marriage for him. Fidelity, maternal instincts and compatibility, that was clearly what he wanted in a wife. Eventually. When the time was right he'd start looking for her. And she didn't have to have shiny brown hair, wide eyes and great legs.

Of course she didn't.

Three days later Frannie's phone rang. She had a mouthful of pins and both hands full, fabric in one hand and scissors in the other, as she bias-cut a beautiful ivory watered silk destined to become an elegant suit for a divorcée who wanted to look lovely but not virginal as she made her second sojourn to the altar.

She scowled at the telephone and decided not to answer it. Let the machine get it, she told herself. It's probably Donald or Robert calling to check up on you. She continued to cut, studiously ignoring each ring, although curiosity and good manners made it difficult for her to resist. What was it about the trill of a telephone that made one hustle to answer it? Was it just her, or did other people have to steel themselves to keep from snatching up the phone? Each time the phone rang, a whole host of possibilities arose.

It might be Oprah, asking her to share her craft with millions of brides via her show.

It might be the Maryland lottery, calling to tell her she would never have to work again...unlikely since she hadn't bought a lottery ticket in her whole life.

It might be Jack, telling her she was the best thing that had ever happened to him, that he couldn't live without her, that he lo— *Whoa!* Where had that come from?

She knew better than to think that she could ever hold the interest of a man who attracted women like red flowers brought hummingbirds in for a sip of nectar. He was just a natural flirt, and she'd been in his line of flirt-fire a few times recently. Plus, she looked especially good right now to a man trying to become an instant parent to an infant. Well, she'd been courted for her adept handling of children before. Her experience with Oliver had taught her what to avoid. As far as she was concerned, Jack might as well be wearing a Wrong Way sign around his neck.

Finally, the machine came on. "You have reached Brooks' Bridals as well as Frannie Brooks. Please leave a message and I will return your call."

Click.

"Hi, Frannie, it's Jack."

Her hand flew to her mouth. Think of the devil, and up he pops.

"If you're free, would you like to come to a barbecue with me next Saturday evening? It's my lacrosse team, and it's a family thing. Casual." His low chuckle vibrated in the air. "I figured this would be a great way to repay your hospitality without having to cook. Am I brilliant or what?"

Brilliant. And handsome and sexy as all get-out. Exactly what I don't need in my life. She reached for the phone and clicked on the receiver, fully intending to decline.

"Hello, Jack."

"Hey, there. My favorite lady. And more importantly, Lex's favorite lady, too."

He couldn't know that his words were an arrow that struck the bull's-eye of her insecurities squarely. But it stiffened her spine, and helped her remember that she was not permitted to throw herself at this man's feet. "Well," she said, assuming her heartiest tone. "It's good to know I'm at the top of somebody's list. Um, Jack, I—"

"You can't say no. It'll be a good time. No pressure, just a friendly kind of thing. C'mon, Frannie." And his tone coaxed her to break her own rules regarding Jack Ferris.

"Maybe just for a little while. I have a busy day again this Saturday and I'll probably be too wiped out to be good company." Dope! You're supposed to tell the man no!

"Great!" His voice rang with enthusiasm, and she could practically feel his pent-up energy through the phone. "How about if I pick you up around four? My lacrosse team's playing the first game of our championship tournament, and the party's afterward. You can relax, prop your feet up at the game and be ready for action later."

She knew it was just his way of saying she'd be rested and refreshed, but a vivid image of his mouth coming down on hers flashed across her mind—

"Or we can go to the party if you're not up for action." He was laughing now, and she had to laugh with him.

"You should be locked up," she said. "Does a day go by that you don't flirt with someone?"

"Not if I can help it." She could still hear a smile in his voice. "So what do you say? Four o'clock on Saturday?"

"All right."

"Okay! See you then." And he hung up.

She stood in the middle of the room, holding the silent receiver. She must be crazy. She'd been going to say that four was too early, that she'd meet him wherever, after his game. But he'd outmaneuvered her. He reminded her of the big, bouncy tiger in one of her favorite children's classics, brimming with boundless energy. But that tiger didn't have a propensity for charming a woman until she forgot all the reasons she shouldn't be going out with him. And that tiger didn't have a sex appeal that erased all common sense and left her pliant and purring at the lightest touch.

She clicked on her phone again, and pressed the numbers of Deirdre's home phone. When the answering machine offered her a chance to speak, she said, "Dee? It's Frannie. Please tell me you don't have plans for Saturday evening. Jack invited me to his lacrosse game and a party, and I want to talk to you! Ask your brother where the game is and be there."

The hours crawled by throughout the rest of the week. Deirdre called to protest that one lacrosse game per season was her limit now, that she didn't have time, that she'd only made that one appearance to satisfy her brother, but Frannie held firm. "I went to court with you when you needed moral support, remember? Even-Steven, sweetie."

Finally it was four o'clock on Saturday. She'd spent an hour, since three, getting ready, which was the silliest thing she'd done in a long while. She never needed an hour. But simple decisions, like what scent to wear and whether or not to add a smidgeon of mascara to her lashes, required major brain cell expenditure this time, and at five minutes before four, she was still transferring Important Female Stuff from one purse to the next. She had barely finished when she heard the growl of a quiet engine turning into her driveway.

She watched from behind her sheer curtains as he unfolded his big frame from his silver sports car. Why in the world did big men insist on driving ridiculous little cars? He couldn't possibly be comfortable in that thing, she thought as he turned and flipped the driver's seat forward, then gently lifted Alexa from her car seat.

He started up the walk. Alexa was cradled in one big arm. He was wearing a blue and gold jersey that clung to the muscles across his chest and her mouth went dry. His gold uniform shorts glowed against his tan and did little to hide the powerful muscles of his thighs and as she looked at the hard, tanned flesh, she whispered, "Oh, my..."

She should have said no.

The doorbell rang. Hurrying toward the door, she slung her purse over her shoulder and grabbed a basket in which she'd stashed a container of brownies she'd made to contribute to the barbecue. "Hi," she said, hating the breathless quality of her voice as she opened the door. "I'm ready to go."

Jack didn't answer. Slowly he extended a hand, silently commanding her to place hers within it. His gaze traveled from the top of her ordinary brown hair, down over the blue-and-white seersucker sundress with its slim crisscross of straps holding up the bodice, down to her whimsical, transparent "jelly" sandals. He cleared his throat. "Did you make your dress?"

She nodded. It always unnerved her when he behaved out of character, and she forced herself not to shuffle her feet. "I make a lot of my own clothing."

"That explains why it fits you so perfectly." He raised his eyes to her face again and she was reassured to see his lighthearted, confident grin spreading again. "I'm going to have to fight off my teammates when they get a look at you."

Now she was worried. "Is it too dressy? I can go and put shorts on." She'd thought the casual dress was the perfect note, but his reaction made her doubt herself.

"Don't you dare. You look great." He released her hand so that she could turn and lock her door, then he surprised her by taking her hand in his and twining her fingers with his as they walked out to the car. "I only meant that I have no intention of sharing you with my teammates or any other man."

I have no intention of sharing you... Dangerous words, if she allowed herself to take them seriously. Which, of, course, she wouldn't. Flirting was as natural to Jack as breathing. It was simply his way of delivering a compliment.

Five

"Jack's an attackman," Deirdre explained. "And the reason our team just got that penalty is because they were offsides."

"Offsides. Is that like outsides or insides?" Frannie snickered at her own wit. Then she caught herself glancing across the bleachers to where Alexa's baby seat sat beside the wife of one of the players for the twentieth time. Jack had explained that one of the other player's wives had volunteered to watch her during the game, and she'd forced herself to resist blurting out an offer to do so herself. And it was the right thing to do, she lectured herself. You are not going to get hoodwinked into taking care of somebody else's child again.

But still... That woman had barely glanced at Alexa since the game began—

"How the heck can you live near Baltimore and know nothing about lacrosse?" Deirdre regarded her as if she were an alien species.

Frannie shrugged. "All my brothers were football and baseball players. Besides, I'm from Taneytown, not Baltimore."

"And it's just up the road." Dee's exasperation changed to an instructional tone as she pointed to the field. "See the line across the middle of the field? It's important. There have to be four men on one side defending the goal and three men attacking the other team's goals. Always. Period. No exceptions. The guys in the middle—the middies—move forward or back depending on whether the attackmen, defensemen or goalie have left their side of the field."

Frannie's eyebrows rose as she concentrated on the game. "Oh! Why didn't you tell me that before? Now it makes sense." She cringed as Jack and a defenseman from the other team appeared to body slam each other in midair, sticks flying with deadly intent. The heavy, "thunking" sound was audible clear up in the bleachers where they sat. "I'll be glad when this is over. I don't think I'd like to watch this time after time like some of the wives."

"You thinking about becoming one of the wives?"

"Sure. Didn't I tell you Jack and I are getting married tomorrow?" Even though she spoke the words in jest, and Deirdre laughed, merely speaking them aloud gave her a funny little tingle. What would it be like to be married to Jack?

Heaven, answered a little voice inside her head.

Forget it, answered another, more practical voice. Wait until you meet a man who wants YOU, not your child-rearing or housekeeping skills.

But what if that man didn't exist? She knew she wasn't a raving beauty. And she wasn't getting any younger.

"...and I didn't send you to Jack's firm with the idea of setting you two up, but now that I see you—"

"What?" She tuned in suddenly to Deirdre's ongoing conversation.

"You're perfect for each other. Jack is a wonderful guy," Dee assured her, eyes serious. Too serious. As serious as they'd been ever since Frannie had known her. "I just never thought he'd settle down again. Of course, the little one makes a difference, too. I know how overwhelming single parenting can be."

"Wait a minute." Settle down again?

Jack had been married?

She forced herself to breathe, despite the sudden weight settling on her chest. Dee was looking at her strangely; she had to get herself together. There was no reason for her to be stunned, upset by the news. "Jack and I are only friends." The words were as much for her as they were for Dee.

Deirdre snorted. "I may not want a man in my life, sweetie, but I am capable of recognizing attraction between two people. Especially two people I know."

Breathing was a little easier. The weight had moved down to the pit of her stomach, although she couldn't dismiss the strange, hollow disappointment that accompanied it. "I've helped him out with the baby a few times and had him over for dinner once. We're just friends."

Dee lifted a brow. "Okay. You don't have to protest so vigorously."

"And as far as I know, Jack isn't thinking of settling down any more than I am. I didn't even know he'd been married." There, she'd sneaked that in pretty neatly. Casual, that was the tone she'd projected.

"Want the scoop?" Dee's smile was smug.

So much for appearing disinterested. "Does grass grow?"

"Well…" Dee crossed one foot over the other and swung her sneakered foot. "Did I mention how grateful I am to my mother for keeping the boys overnight tonight?"

"Twice already."

"And did I mention that Nelson hasn't made a support payment in more than six months."

"Monthly update."

"How about—"

"Dee!"

"Oh, right. What can I tell you about the former Mrs. Ferris...?" She tapped her chin, then relented when Frannie gave her a fierce glare. "Her name was Lannette and Jack dated her his senior year in college. They were inseparable from the day they met. Made all of his friends gag. You know, that lovebird behavior people do when they're infatuated?"

Frannie nodded. This should not be making her feel so miserable.

"They got married in June, right after they graduated, and they were together for five years. Jack worshiped the ground she walked on. I can remember my brother being really disgusted because Jack wouldn't go anywhere without her. I don't think his friends particularly cared for her."

"Why not?" Gossiping was a nasty business, she lectured herself, and she should stop right now.

She leaned forward so she could hear Dee better over the cheering of the people behind them.

"She seemed very self-centered to me, but I only met her twice. Once at the wedding, and one other time. Anyway, I don't really know what happened, but I do know she was the one who left. And I guess they were divorced shortly after that."

She couldn't imagine leaving Jack if he belonged to her. The woman must have been mentally ill.

Around them, fans were beginning to clomp down over the bleachers. The game was over, and she realized she didn't even know who had won. She looked out over the field toward the benches and caught Jack watching her. When he saw that she had seen him, he waved and beckoned. But for a moment, before he'd smiled, she thought she'd seen the same taut expression he'd worn the night he'd kissed her in his bedroom. Almost an angry one, although she couldn't fathom what she might have done.

Before the little voice in her head could give her another lecture, she retrieved Alexa from the baby-sitting team wife and carried her down to the grass. Jack started toward her, stopping for a quick word or a hug and a smile for people he passed...women people, she thought to herself. The man was a doggone magnet. He met her at the foot of the bleachers, reaching for the shoulder strap of the diaper bag and slinging it over his shoulder with his duffle. Placing an arm about Frannie's waist, he escorted her toward the parking lot.

"Hi, gorgeous. Did you miss me?" His gray eyes snagged her gaze, sending a warm message of intimacy that made her shiver involuntarily as he bent toward her. For one heart-stopping instant, she thought he intended to kiss her. Then she realized he was only leaning close to inspect Alexa, who was still sleeping.

Breaking the eye contact, she deliberately chose to misinterpret his words. "If she missed you, she's not telling."

His grin flashed, but he didn't call her on the evasion. "Don't you want to stroke my ego?"

She laughed. "A million women fall for your nonsense every day. Your ego doesn't need any help from me."

"Are you sure?" The look he shot her was suddenly very serious, very un-Jacklike. Hardly the silly retort she'd expected.

It shook her right down to the tips of her sandals. She didn't know how to respond, and in any case, her tongue felt as if it were tangled in a big knot. So she didn't say anything at all.

Why had he asked that in That Tone, with That Look? It implied a deeper relationship than the casual friendship she was determined to maintain. She was terrified by the notion that she might mean something more to him than simply another female friend, because if he continued to treat her as if she were special, she'd never be able to resist him.

And she'd be darned if she'd fall for him. She liked her life just fine, thank you, and she didn't need to foul up her peace with another case of heartbreak.

Sooner or later a broken heart would be the end result of any relationship with Jack.

They had reached the car. He propped himself against it and switched shoes, since the heavy spikes were strictly for grass playing fields, then stowed his gear in the trunk.

One of the other players approached and said, "Hey, Ferris. Mind stopping for a couple bottles of soda on the way over? Tammy thinks we don't have enough."

"No problem. See you in fifteen." The other man walked on to another vehicle while Jack opened her door for her, then took Alexa so he could put her in her car seat. As he started the engine, he asked, "Did Janet feed her or change her during the game?"

Relieved to have the conversation back on a safer footing, she said, "She said she fed her eight ounces during the last quarter of the game. Alexa's been asleep since then."

"Great." His smile was wry. "She'll be wide-awake and ready for action at the barbecue."

The drive to the home of the couple having the party was short after a brief stop at a convenience store for the sodas. Jack parked the car in a long row of others, one of two that lined each side of the street in front of a brick-and-siding bilevel. The siding was a startling shade of green. As they started up the driveway to the rear of the home, Jack leaned close. "You get a prize for not doing a double take at that color."

She couldn't help smiling. "It certainly is... unforgettable."

"You must have been a diplomat in your last life. Stuart is color-blind. He picked it out himself while Tammy and the kids were away on a family visit, and he painted it as a surprise for her."

"What a surprise!"

"Yeah. But Tammy's a great gal. She's never told him it's less than perfect. To this day, Stu thinks he gave his wife a great welcome-home gift."

"That's so sweet." She giggled. "How many years will it be before she can have it painted again without hurting his feelings?"

He laughed as they rounded the corner of the house. "I don't know. He only—"

"Surprise!"

Jack stopped dead.

Everyone had gotten there ahead of them, thanks to the baby and the soda stop. Attached to the chairs and tables were dozens of pink balloons, and a table straight ahead was bedecked in pink crepe paper streamers. It bore a pretty flower arrangement and a huge cake trimmed in pink. Gifts were piled beneath the table.

"Come to your baby shower, Jack." A plump little woman with deep dimples came forward and took his hand, winking at Frannie. "We thought you could use a little help getting ready for the baby, even if she did arrive first."

"You guys...you guys are really something." Jack shook his head and scrubbed his free hand down over his face. She could tell he was touched; a tenderness seized her as he wiped away a tear. Only a man who was strong and secure could allow himself to shed a tear in front of other guys. She suspected he'd be teased later, but for now, the men coming forward to shake his hand and congratulate him on becoming a "father" wore genuinely kind expressions.

Rats. Rats, rats, and more rats. A man who could let himself cry was the sexiest thing on earth. Although she'd never tell him that.

"Did you know about this?" he demanded.

"Of course not. These people didn't even know you'd be bringing me along."

"But we're delighted to meet you." The dimpled woman held out her hand as Jack was engulfed and guided over to the table. "Hi, I'm Tammy, the one who got drafted into organizing this party. Men are great at coming up with

ideas, but they stink when it comes to details.'' Her dimples
dug deep grooves in her cheeks.

"It's nice to meet you. I'm Frannie.''

"Oh, you're the one!'' Tammy turned and at the top of
her considerable lungs, announced, "This is Frannie. She's
the one Jack's been talking about.''

"Ah-ha. The Mystery Woman.'' A tall man whose bright
blue shirt and aqua shorts told her who he was before he
spoke, came over to lead her to a chair. "I'm Stu, your
host.''

The one he talked about? The mystery woman? She
squirmed uncomfortably as what seemed like a thousand
pairs of eyes assessed her. She knew he'd been grateful for
her help, but she had no idea he'd told everyone in Butler
County.

As Jack's friends and teammates included her in the circle of banter, she began to relax. These people were genuinely enjoyable. She couldn't remember the last time she'd
laughed so much.

They ate and they lounged. Men told jokes and helped
their wives referee spats between the various children
bouncing around; mothers mopped up little faces. The team
members told tales on each other, and before Frannie knew
it, Tammy was passing out cake and directing her troops
to eat while Jack opened the presents. Someone dragged a
chair forward and Tammy set the first box in his lap. The
tips of his ears turned pink.

She'd never have believed it, but Jack was embarrassed.

"Now I know how uncomfortable women feel at these
things,'' he said. "Why does everybody have to watch?''

Stu laughed. "Because this is what you do at showers.
Right?''

"Right!'' chorused a host of female voices.

"So stop stallin' and start rippin','' added one.

Once he got into the swing, Jack played his role with
zeal, flinging wrap and ribbon into the air, oohing and aah-
ing over teeny ruffled sleepers and frilly dresses. He was

fascinated by a specially designed bucket that sealed dirty diapers within a plastic casing, and he'd have tried it out right there if they'd let him. Receiving blankets, little sheets, a mobile to hang over the crib, board books, stuffed animals, the pile of opened gifts grew until there was only one box left.

Jack roared with laughter as soon as he removed the lid from the box.

"Let's see!"

"What is it?"

"C'mon, Ferris, show everybody!"

Still chuckling, Jack reached into the box. The room erupted in laughter from the men and cooing from the women as he held up a miniature lacrosse stick complete with pocket, and a tiny pair of spiked sneakers sporting pink bows. "This is great!" he said with real delight, "But is it the legal size?"

"Three-minute penalty for short stick!" shouted one of the guys.

"That's adorable," said a tall, tanned blonde. "I'm glad somebody remembered that lacrosse isn't just a men's sport."

"Ah, we just let you gals play to make you feel better—" And the room erupted into another round of raucous insults and laughter.

The gift giving concluded, and people began to gather children from the swing set at the far end of the yard and pack up the empty dishes they had brought. Several of the men staggered out to Jack's car to load the gifts as he thanked Stu and Tammy.

Stu slapped him on the shoulder. "Think nothing of it, buddy. Hey, are you going to be able to make that charity tournament on the seventh? I need three more guys to make up a team, and I hate to let them down."

Jack hesitated. "Better not count on me. I'm having a heck of a time finding a good sitter for Lex and—"

"Oh, come on. I'd hate to have to cancel."

"All right. Let me see what I can work out and I'll let you know."

"Tomorrow."

"I'll let you know," Jack repeated.

"Frannie." Stu's eyes lit up as he turned to her, a clear appeal in his voice. "Could you help him out? You could consider it a charitable contribution."

"Hey, wait a minute," Jack protested. "Frannie doesn't baby-sit."

"Actually," she said, "I'm already booked that day. I'm keeping my nephews in Taneytown." And it was true.

"So you could take the baby along." Stu had it all worked out.

"I don't think—" She'd sworn she wasn't going to let Jack take advantage of her.

"Please? The team needs you. I need you. Jack needs you."

It was for a good cause, she told herself. And Jack wasn't the one who was asking. Slowly she said, "I guess I could take her along."

It would have been nice if Jack had protested immediately, if he'd refused to allow her to get involved in his child care problems. But Jack was silent, looking at her with a strangely unreadable expression on his face.

"Fantastic!" Stu put his arm around her and steered her toward Jack's car, oblivious to the atmosphere he'd created in the air.

This shower stuff was exhausting, Jack thought. It was worse than playing back-to-back games. He glanced over at Frannie, unable to make out much more than her profile in the darkness that had finally overtaken the long summer day.

She'd seemed comfortable among his pals and their families. And they'd certainly taken to her. Lannette had never liked his friends, many of whom he'd known since they played lacrosse together in high school or college. And though they'd been too polite to say it, he knew they hadn't been fond of her, either.

Wow, he must be tired, he thought. He rarely thought of his ex-wife anymore. He'd licked his wounds in private after she'd left him, and gradually they had healed. And he'd gotten smarter. When he was younger, he'd thought marriage and love meant sharing everything, meant that your best friend was the person with whom you shared the rest of your life. Meant that your heart was held in another's care.

Lannette hadn't wanted his heart, except maybe as a trophy. She didn't have it in her to share of herself, to really care about him or anybody else. All they'd shared was passion, and it was his own stupid fault he'd made himself believe they shared more. Ah, nuts to the past. Why was he thinking about that when he had a woman like Frannie sitting beside him?

He turned the car onto her street and pulled to a stop in her driveway, then turned to her. What would she do if he simply leaned across the space between them and took her mouth? He'd been watching her at the party. As she delicately licked the last of the creamy icing from her fork, she'd glanced up at him. Those luscious lips had curved into a sweet smile and he'd very nearly dropped his drink. He couldn't forget the physical longing that had rushed through him; just thinking about it now stirred his desire.

He didn't want the evening to end. Or if it had to, he wanted it to end with Frannie coming home with him, going through all the bedtime rituals he'd established with Lex, and then, after she slept, coming into his bed. He didn't believe in love anymore like he had when he'd been a callow kid, but he was beginning to think of other reasons why marriage could be a good idea. Frannie would be the perfect wife for him.

Wife? Was he going crazy? He'd decided he could get along just fine without ever going through the marriage mess again. Hadn't he already decided he wasn't looking for a wife?

He was only considering the idea because he felt so strongly that a child needed two parents. That was the only reason he was thinking so much about Frannie.

But she wasn't interested. Or at least she wasn't interested in acting on the exciting charge of awareness that zipped through them both each time their eyes met. He knew she felt it, too. There was no way this could be all one-sided.

What made her so wary? She was like a mistreated cat, dying to purr and rub herself against him, but a little too afraid to come within reach. He had the feeling sometimes that she was thinking of someone else when she looked at him—someone that had left a bad taste in her mouth.

Well, he wasn't that someone, and he wasn't going to let her get away with thinking of anyone else anymore.

She put her hand on the door, ready to open it herself if he didn't get moving, so he got out and came around to pull hers open. But then, some imp within him refused to let him step back and behave like a gentleman. Things were moving way too slowly with her; he'd stir up the waters and see what happened.

"Thanks for coming with me. I know it was a bit overwhelming for a first date."

She had been making rustling sounds as she reached behind the seat for her purse and the doggie bag of cake Tammy had insisted she take along. The noises stopped abruptly.

"It wasn't a first date," she said.

He read doubt in her tone, and he wondered who she was trying to convince—him or herself. "That's right, it was a second."

"It was not a date."

"I know, I know, we're just friends." He could see her face now, softly lit by moonlight, her eyes troubled as she looked up at him, and he put his hands on her shoulders, gently massaging the delicate flesh. "Then how come I don't feel like 'just a friend'?"

Her body had gone stiff at the first touch of his hands; she stood like a statue before him. "I don't know," she whispered, but in her eyes he could see that she knew as well as he did what was happening between them. It was the end of his restraint.

Bending his head, he set his mouth on hers as he'd been dreaming of doing for weeks, since he'd first tasted her the night of the hospital jaunt. At the same time, he took her arms and lifted them to his shoulders, then put his around her and drew her fully against him. On tiptoe, she leaned into him, not rejecting the caresses. Even though he'd initiated the intimacy, was prepared for the feel of her body, he inhaled sharply. Her breasts felt resilient and yielding; the vee where her legs met was the perfect cradle for his rapidly growing male flesh. Her lips were soft and pliant under his and she began to return his kisses. The quest for satisfaction roared through him and he tightened his embrace.

He turned with her in his arms and braced his back against the car. His legs spread wide for balance; her body pressed between them. As she moved to put her arms more firmly around his neck, her body shifted and rubbed over his and his breath exploded in harsh pleasure.

It took every ounce of control he had to keep the kiss from becoming the wild uncontrollable thing that raged inside him. Instead, he angled his mouth more fully over hers and began to touch the very edges of her lips with his tongue, light, gentle tracings that encouraged her to participate. And to his elation, she did.

Her mouth opened to allow him access. Although her tongue wasn't bold enough to stroll out and dance with his at first, it was waiting for his invitation. Within moments, the gentle kisses weren't enough. She moaned under his mouth as he plunged his tongue deep in a pseudo mating that mimicked what he really wanted—her under him, naked and clinging as he rode her....

But he couldn't sustain conscious thought. Her hips were twisting slowly against him now and his hard, aching flesh pulsed with a life of its own as her body pressed back and forth from side to side. Her breasts pushed at his chest. He put up a hand and cupped one through the bodice of the little sundress that had been teasing him all night, and she gave a small cry that was stifled beneath his mouth. But she didn't push him away. He immediately transferred his attention to the satiny skin along her jaw, to the warm, fragrant hollow of her throat, and his thumb brushed the tip of her breast until the tiny hard nub of her nipple stood up. She said something in a faint tone that he didn't catch, and against her throat he muttered, "What?"

"We're just friends."

He really hated to interrupt this, but it was time she understood. Lifting his head, he caught her gaze in the dim light, holding it as he spoke deliberately. "In case you haven't figured it out yet, we aren't 'just friends' anymore. I don't know what we are, but I like it. And so do you." He lowered his head to her mouth again, nibbling lightly at one corner. "Tell me you like it."

"I like it," she whispered. But as he lowered his head again, she tore her mouth from his and brought her hand up to pull his away from her breast. "But I'm not sure this is smart."

"Maybe not," he conceded, moving his hand to her buttocks and rubbing her back and forth over the hard ridge distorting the shape of his uniform shorts, "Sure is fun, though. Don't you think it's fun?"

She laughed, but it was almost a painful sound. "*Fun* isn't the word I would use to describe this. I have to think." Taking his arms, she pulled with determination until, with a deep sigh for the night that could have been, he slowly released her.

He sighed and rested his forehead against hers, resigned to a long, cold shower and a colder bed. "Why?"

"Because...just because." She allowed him to steal one more soft kiss before he lifted his head.

His hands rested loosely on the soft swell of her hips. Stepping back, he waited while she gathered her things, then took her hand and walked her the short distance to the door.

She dug in her purse for her key and unlocked the door, then turned to face him. Her face was a study in consternation, he thought, freshly aroused by the way she chewed her bottom lip. He'd seen her do it before and it got to him every time. Of course, there wasn't much about her he could think of that didn't get to him.

Putting a finger under her chin, he said, "Don't look so worried."

"Why not?" She sounded belligerent and almost tearful, and she kept her eyes on the placket of his shirt. "We were doing fine just being friends. This changes everything."

"I know," he soothed. "You need some time to get used to this. But, Frannie—" he paused and waited until she looked up at him "—we weren't meant to be only friends. This was bound to happen, and I can't say I'm sorry, because I'm not." He smiled briefly and gathered her to him, kissing her deeply one last time and waiting until she responded before he let her go. "And if you're honest with yourself, you aren't sorry, either."

No, she wasn't sorry, she thought two days later. How could she be sorry that Jack had kissed her, touched her like she was the only woman alive? How could she be sorry that he so clearly wanted her?

He'd indicated his interest several times, but she'd forced herself to believe he was only practicing his charm on her. After the other night, she couldn't pretend anymore. He'd torn a huge hole in her denial and deliberately ripped it even wider when he clarified his position.

She knew he wanted her. There was no question that she wanted him. No question at all, she thought, her body reacting to the memory of his lips and hands on her body, his hard, demanding strength pressed against her. When Jack pulled her into his arms, she turned into a quivering lump of willing flesh that begged, "Mold me, shape me."

But she still wasn't sure it was smart. Maybe she should call a halt to this before she couldn't.

And that, she thought, was the sixty-four-thousand-dollar question.

Could she?

He'd called yesterday, and though they'd talked of nothing important, there had been a new intimacy in his deep tones. If she was honest with herself, she'd admit that she couldn't simply walk away. She was afraid, yes. Afraid that he was coming to mean far too much to her. She thought she'd been in love once before, but it had turned to dust. Loving Jack would mean keeping her vision clear, remembering that he didn't return the feeling.

She'd better have her eyes checked, then, because she had a bad feeling that it was too late for decisions. Her heart had followed her body into his arms Saturday night.

He hadn't asked to see her again until next weekend, when she'd let Stu coerce her into taking Alexa to Taneytown with her. Already she was dreading a whole week away from him, and it was only Monday evening.

The doorbell rang. She wasn't expecting company, and she frowned slightly. She was in the middle of mopping the kitchen floor, and it went against her nature to stop in the middle of the job.

Setting aside the mop, she wiped her hands on the ratty old jean shorts she'd put on for the task, and went to the front door. She slipped off the dead bolt and opened the door.

Jack stood on the porch, with Alexa cradled in one arm. Her heart bounded into a joyous dance, and she knew a silly smile had plastered itself over her face. "Hi." Her voice was quiet; if she expressed the feelings running through her, the whole neighborhood would get an earful.

"Hi." His eyes were warm and dancing with silver lights. He returned the smile. "Can I come in?"

"Of course." She stepped back, feeling ridiculous. How could this man send every shred of her common sense on vacation?

"I wanted to talk to you about something." As he stepped past her, she felt seared by the close proximity. Then he turned to face her as she closed the door.

For a long moment he simply studied her face.

"What?" she asked. Jack wasn't normally one to hesitate. The way he was examining her features began to make her wonder if she should have cleaned her face rather than the kitchen floor.

"I want to talk to you," he repeated. Then, reaching out, he slipped one big hand beneath her hair and gently clasped the back of her neck. "But I don't think we're going to be able to talk until we've gotten this out of the way."

This time, when he reached for her, there was no hesitation in her response. She couldn't have resisted if there'd been a million dollars riding on it. She let him draw her against him with his free arm, let him kiss her, kissed him back. Hadn't she been thinking of this for the past forty-eight hours?

His hand slipped from her nape slowly down her back, over the smooth swell of her buttocks, and pulled her firmly against him. Angled against his side as she was, his knee slipped easily between her legs as he pushed her higher, closer, until she was riding his thigh, wriggling slightly and moaning into his mouth when he turned slightly so that she could feel him, erect and engorged, against the very spot that ached for his possession.

There was no thought in her head of stopping, no thought in her head of any kind. She was his, to touch and taste as he willed, thrilling to the heavy, muscled flesh beneath her palms and between her legs.

The Silhouette Reader Service® — Here's how it works:

Accepting your 2 free books and mystery gift places you under no obligation to buy anything. You may keep the books and gift and return the shipping statement marked "cancel." If you do not cancel, about a month later we'll send you 6 additional novels and bill you just $3.12 each in the U.S., or $3.49 in Canada, plus 25¢ delivery per book and applicable taxes if any.* That's the complete price and — compared to the cover price of $3.75 in the U.S. and $4.25 in Canada — it's quite a bargain! You may cancel at any time, but if you choose to continue, every month we'll send you 6 more books, which you may either purchase at the discount price or return to us and cancel your subscription.

*Terms and prices subject to change without notice. Sales tax applicable in N.Y. Canadian residents will be charged applicable provincial taxes and GST.

If offer card is missing write to: Silhouette Reader Service, 3010 Walden Ave., P.O. Box 1867, Buffalo NY 14240-1867

NO POSTAGE
NECESSARY
IF MAILED
IN THE
UNITED STATES

BUSINESS REPLY MAIL
FIRST-CLASS MAIL   PERMIT NO. 717   BUFFALO, NY

POSTAGE WILL BE PAID BY ADDRESSEE

SILHOUETTE READER SERVICE
3010 WALDEN AVE
PO BOX 1867
BUFFALO NY 14240-9952

But Jack apparently retained the ability to think. The hard steel of his arm around her gradually lessened the demanding pressure, allowing her to slide down to the floor. The action had her shivering all over in response to the sensation, and she couldn't bring herself to move her body away from the firm contact with his. His mouth reduced the deep, thrilling kisses to smaller and smaller ones that barely brushed her lips.

When he lifted his head, there was regret in his eyes. "There are definitely times when a baby gets in the way."

The baby! She'd completely forgotten that he still cradled Alexa in his other arm. Heat flared in her face as she stepped back and mustered a shaky laugh, slipping her hands under the infant and lifting her into her arms. "Maybe it's a good thing. My brain shuts down when you're around."

"Good." There was a wealth of smug satisfaction in his prompt reply. "I like it when you can't think. You managed to keep me at arm's length for six weeks with that brain clicking away. Is there a switch?"

Why dissemble at this point? You practically told him he can have you any time he chooses. "I guess you've found it."

He regarded her with a look of pure male possession, clearly satisfied with her answer. "I guess so."

Alexa stirred in Frannie's arms, and she remembered that he'd just walked in the door. "Would you like a drink?" she asked. "You caught me cleaning and I'm ready for a break." Liar. She'd always been one to charge right through housecleaning nonstop until she got it done.

"I can think of things I'd like better, but I'll settle for a beer," he answered. "Mind if I lay a blanket down for Lex?"

"Sure. But I don't have any beer. I have—" she paused and ruefully catalogued the contents of her refrigerator "—lemonade, nonfat milk, iced tea, cooking wine and good old H_2O. April and I are usually the only ones around,'' she said as explanation. ''I'm not much of a drinker.''

''Iced tea will be fine.'' He spread out a soft baby blanket, and Frannie knelt to lay Alexa gently on it before escaping to the refuge of her kitchen. Where is this going? she asked herself as she poured the tea with hands that shook. She hadn't intended to fall for Jack Ferris; in fact, she'd expressly decided she wasn't going to care for him. But choice didn't seem to be an option anymore. He'd declared war on her senses, and she'd surrendered before any real skirmish even could take place.

She hadn't wanted to love him, but she did. She loved him. The shaking in her hands spread to her entire body. She gripped the edge of the counter with both hands and took a deep breath, willing herself to calm. She might not be able to resist loving him, but she wasn't a complete idiot. There wasn't even a hope that he felt the same. Oh, he desired her—that much was obvious now. But he didn't love her.

And he couldn't be allowed to know she loved him.

Six

Jack wondered what she was going to think of his idea. Instinct told him she would refuse the offer, but he was determined to do it, anyway. She'd already helped him with Alexa far more than he could ever hope to repay her for. If she wouldn't take money, he'd try another angle.

She was taking a long time getting a simple glass of tea. Maybe she was fixing herself up, combing her hair and putting some lipstick on, the way women always did when you caught them looking less than completely put together. He didn't mind that she'd had her hair pulled away from her face with a wide hairband, that she wasn't wearing any makeup. He'd learned the hard way that how a woman looked didn't necessarily offer insight into her character. Lannette had been a beautifully put-together package. It had taken him a long, long time to see that what lay beneath the surface wasn't beautiful as well.

Lex gurgled in that funny little way she'd just started, and he leaned over the blanket. She lay on her back, her eyes wide and fascinated with the hands attached to the ends of her arms. It tickled him immensely to see the little ways she was growing and changing, and he laughed silently at himself. Stu had told him at the surprise party that he would have never believed Jack would be so good with a baby if he hadn't seen it with his own eyes.

"One of those in your arms really suits you, buddy," Stu had said, shaking his head in wonder.

One of these really did suit him, he thought. He'd been marking time in his life, just drifting. The only thing he'd been sure of was that he would never let another woman have the kind of power over him that Lannette had had. And then Lex had been dropped on him. It had been a nightmare at first. Then, when he'd gotten his balance back, it had become a challenge. He could be just as good a father as any of his buddies.

Now it was an addiction. Alexa was his child. It was that simple.

Frannie walked back into the room then, interrupting his reverie. She carried a small tray with two tall glasses filled with tea and clinking ice cubes, and a plate of what looked like raisin cookies. Above the tray, which she carried waist high, her breasts bobbed gently. He'd noticed the minute she opened the door that she wasn't wearing any bra beneath the tank top; when she'd pressed up against him, the feel of those firm, yielding mounds shouted at him to touch.

Below the tray, her legs were long and tanned, with shapely calves and slender ankles. The muscles in her thighs flexed as she moved and he felt a corresponding response in his own body. The kiss at the door hadn't been nearly enough, as far as he was concerned. Still, the way she'd come into his arms, like she'd been waiting for him to reach for her, was enough to keep him going for a little while.

She set the tray down and handed him a glass, and he took her hand and drew her down on the blanket beside him. "Check this out," he said. "She's figured out she has hands."

Frannie laughed. "I love this stage."

"So far, I've liked all her stages," he said. "Or, at least, I have since I got a handle on this dad thing. I can't wait to see her grow up."

"Yes, you can. If you live through the toddler stage, then you'll get a double whammy when she turns into an adolescent."

He grinned. "Oh, well. My life was pretty dull before this, anyway." He reached over and curled his fingers around hers where they lay on her knee. "It's gotten a whole lot better recently."

She smiled. Then she turned her palm up and squeezed his fingers gently, before scooting away and taking a seat on the low ottoman on the other side of the blanket. It wasn't a rejection, exactly, but it definitely was a "back off," notice. Not a chance, he told her mentally. But he didn't say it aloud. What she didn't know could only be to his advantage.

"I'd like to get your thoughts on an idea I had," he told her.

Her eyebrows rose, and he knew she was wondering why he needed her input. "All right."

He took a deep breath. "I know you don't want to be paid for helping me with Alexa, but I'd like to do something for you—" He held up a hand when she started to protest. "I have this friend, a photographer. He offered me a photo shoot in exchange for a favor I did him a few months ago. I haven't needed to collect so far, and I got to thinking that maybe you could use two or three professional shots for the walls in your shop."

"Jack, I couldn't possibly accept something like that. Professional photography sessions cost a fortune."

"This one's free," he pointed out.

"I know, but—"

"And he wants me to use it right away because he's getting busy with senior portraits and he wants to get it finished first. You'd be doing me a favor, actually."

"How so?" She still looked like she was going to refuse.

"I haven't been happy with the photographer I use for the business, and I've been thinking of making a change. This will give me a chance to see if I like Runt's work enough to switch to him."

"Runt?" she repeated. "Poor guy."

Jack laughed. "You won't pity him once you meet him." He eyed her, trying to gauge her response to his proposition. "So will you do it?"

"I...don't know. I really don't feel comfortable accepting payment for helping you with Alexa. Snuggling a baby again was payment."

He sighed. This was even more difficult than he'd expected. "If you won't let me do this, I'm going to bug you until you let me pay you. Look at it this way—if you do this photo shoot for me, we'll never have to have this conversation again."

Her eyes were locked on his face, and for a moment he forgot he was waiting for an answer. What was it about her that he couldn't resist? She was quietly pretty, but he'd dated women more beautiful. She had a nice figure, but he'd dated women whose curves literally would stop traffic.

But she projected something...it was like the air around her was scented with her own invisible come-to-me perfume. All he wanted was to reach across the space dividing them and haul her into his lap. And proceed from there. With haste.

"It would be very nice."

He blinked, momentarily disoriented. "Wha—it would?"

She nodded. "If you're sure—"

"I'm sure. It's one of those use-it-or-lose-it situations."

"Actual photos of my designs would be wonderful." She was beginning to look more enthusiastic. He had her hooked.

"Great. I'll talk to him and then call you. We can work out a time. Do you want to line up a model or shall I?"

"A model?"

"I have the perfect girl in mind, I use her frequently. Never mind, I'll take care of it."

"You move fast when you decide to move, don't you?" She shook her head, a bemused smile playing around her lips.

He couldn't resist. "You should know."

She blushed. He was astonished. He'd never seen Frannie truly unsettled like this before. She usually was the epitome of poise and self-possession. Nothing much seemed to faze her.

She wouldn't look at him, but focused on the baby, who was beginning to squeal and squeak. Frannie's rosy cheeks were adorable. He had to sit firmly on the urge to lean over and kiss her until they were both crazy for more.

Instead, he shifted and reached for the diaper bag. "That sounds like the prelude to the 'Feed Me Fast' opera. Could I impose on you to warm up a bottle while I change her?"

She smiled at him, blush forgotten now that she was on familiar ground. "Why don't you warm the bottle? I'd love to change her."

"Be my guest." He rose. "I could live happily without handling another diaper in this life."

He heated the formula in a cup of hot water from the tap. When he judged it warm enough, he hurried back into the living room. Lex wasn't screaming yet, but he expected the serenade to start any minute now.

But she wasn't even fussing. Frannie stood near her small fireplace with the baby in her arms. She was looking down into the tiny face, speaking in a quiet, earnest tone, and he could see one wildly waving infant hand trying to zero in on the fascinating person speaking.

She was made for motherhood.

The thought didn't surprise him. But what did catch him off guard was the deep longing for this intimate scene to be his. He hadn't minded living alone since Lannette. And even when he was married, he'd never spent any time like this. Lannette hated to be stuck at home with no pressing plans. With him.

Schooling his face into what he hoped was an unrevealing expression to hide the dark thoughts bouncing around in his head, he walked over to them. "Here's her bottle. Would you like to feed her?"

"I'd love to." Frannie's voice was fervent. Taking the bottle of formula, she settled into the rocking chair by the hearth with the baby cradled in one arm. Recognizing the position, Alexa immediately began to fuss, but she quieted the instant the nipple was placed against her lips. With lusty sucking sounds, she relaxed and began to drain the bottle.

Jack dropped into the easy chair, watching Frannie's face. She loved babies, that was certain, and she seemed to love his baby in particular.

"I wish I could find someone who would care for her like you do to keep her," he said.

Frannie's head shot up. "You haven't found a baby-sitter yet?" Incredulity laced her tone and her eyes were wide and disbelieving.

He shook his head. "Not yet. But I'm still trying."

"What do you do with her while you're at work?"

He shrugged. "She comes along."

"What?"

Her tone made him feel strangely defensive. "It isn't easy but I'm managing—"

"Your office is no place for a baby. What do you do with her while you're in meetings?"

"I keep her with me."

"In your office? With clients?"

He spread his hands. "What else can I do? It's getting crazier now because she isn't sleeping as much as she did a month ago."

"And she's only going to be awake more and more as she grows." Frannie's gaze was intense. "Jack, you have to get a caregiver for this baby."

"I know." He exhaled heavily and let his head drop back

against the chair, addressing the ceiling. "But I've interviewed almost twenty-five people and none of them seemed right. I just can't leave her with a perfect stranger, whether it's in my home or someone else's. We're on the waiting list at two day care centers that I thought were well staffed and caring, but they're both full and I'm not even at the top of the list. The directors tell me it could be months before a space opens up."

"You can't possibly keep taking her to work with you for months."

"I don't have a choice, Frannie." He glanced at her, and the look on her face arrested his gaze. "Unless you've changed your mind about keeping her?"

The bottle had slipped out of Alexa's mouth; the baby was slumbering against Frannie's breast. Gently she lifted the infant and laid her over her shoulder, rubbing the little back lightly. At his words, Frannie closed her eyes. Turning her face, she nuzzled against the baby with her cheek.

Then an immense sigh shook her and she opened her eyes. "I can't stand the thought of just anyone handling her. I suppose I could keep her until a space in a reputable day care facility becomes available."

Jubilation danced a jig within him, but he fought not to show it on his face. Humble gratitude was a better posture, given the magnitude of her offer. "Are you sure? I'd be delighted, but I don't want to take advantage of you." At least, not in the baby-sitting department.

"I'm sure." She took the baby from her shoulder and cradled the limp form in her arms again. "My busiest season is ending. I have one assistant—who loves babies, by the way—and I'm interviewing for a second one to start training. I think for the short term, I'm better equipped than you are to fit her into my routine." Then she shook her finger at him in warning. "But this is only a temporary arrangement."

He nodded. "I'll call the day care places every week to check on the list. They'll get so sick of hearing from me that they'll fit her in just to get me to quit calling." He hesitated for a second, weighing his next words. "You'll have to let me reimburse you for your time, as I would any caregiver—"

"Jack." Her voice was firm and intense. "I will not take your money, and if you bring it up again, I will not keep Alexa." She paused and glared at him. "Deal?"

He knew better than to argue when she was in that mode. But, God, he loved it when she got on her high horse. When her eyebrows formed that straight, fierce line, his body formed its own straight, fierce line, telling him exactly how to smooth out her furrowed brow. "Deal."

He brought over a portable crib, an infant seat and what seemed like ten tons of baby supplies on Tuesday evening, as well as a wind-up swing he'd purchased on the way over to her house. He'd gotten one shortly after Alexa came to live with him, and the thing was a charm.

Frannie held the baby while he carried the stuff into her house. Then she directed him through to her workroom, where he set up the swing and deposited the baby seat. The crib went in a corner of her kitchen, which was attached to the shop, and he attached a bright mobile above it before laying Lex inside to see how she liked the bright colors revolving in the air above her.

"That way, I'll be able to hear her when she wakes up, but she'll be able to nap without any distractions," she told him as they watched Alexa's eyes follow the mobile.

"Speaking of distractions…" He hooked an arm around her waist and pulled her against him. He'd done his best to keep his hands off her, not an easy task when his body told him to touch her every chance he got. But Lannette had hated having him touching her all the time. She'd complained constantly that she needed "more space," that he was crowding her.

So he had resisted the urge to sit beside Frannie on the couch and cuddle her in one arm while she fed Lex last night, and he'd disciplined himself not to leap on her like a starving wolf the minute she opened the door this evening...the way he had last night.

But he couldn't wait any longer to feel her soft curves against him again.

He heaved a sigh of warm relief at the sweet feel of her as he closed the distance between their bodies, and he felt the thrust of his masculine flesh cushioned by yielding female. "How come I can't stop thinking about you?"

"I don't know." She leaned back in his arms and placed her palms against his chest. The action plastered her lower body more tightly against him, and he knew she couldn't miss his arousal throbbing against her belly. Her velvety eyes were dark and mysterious, unreadable as she gazed up at him in the brightly lit kitchen. "I can't stop thinking about you, either."

The admission pleased him enormously; he could practically feel his chest swelling like Tarzan. Come to think of it, he felt like picking her up and carrying her off, too. Her palms were caressing small circles over the broad planes of his chest, and his hips surged against her of their own accord. Slowly he lowered his head, searching for her mouth. He kept his eyes open, locked on hers until her lashes fluttered down and she lifted herself on tiptoe, pressing her lips to his in an unmistakable offering.

Without hesitation, he sought her tongue with his while his hands roamed up and down her back and buttocks. She clasped her arms around his neck. One hand cradled his skull, holding his mouth to hers. And, that suddenly, he knew how this evening had to end.

God, he felt like he was going to explode. Right here in her kitchen. Tearing his mouth away from hers, he muttered, "I want you. Now."

Her eyes widened, startled, he supposed, at his frank statement.

He glanced at the crib, and her gaze followed his. Alexa had fallen asleep, little arms and legs flung wide in a dream's embrace. He felt like a kid sneaking off with his girl in the back seat of his parents' car, with Time the enemy, as he bent his head and crushed her lips beneath his again. He slipped one hand beneath her, lifting her into even greater contact with his aching flesh. The other hand caught one bare thigh and pulled it high around his waist, caressing the long, satiny length of leg. All that stood between them were a few flimsy layers of fabric. His fingers slipped beneath the edge of the shorts she wore, sliding beneath the elastic at the leg of her panties. He clasped her naked bottom and she jolted in his arms, a husky moan escaping into his mouth. The satiny feel of her skin was both heaven and hell.

"Where's your bedroom?" He barely recognized the deep, hoarse voice as his own.

She hesitated.

He lifted her off her one supporting leg and pulled it up to wrap around his hips with the other, and began to walk toward the steps at the front of the house. "The bed is optional. This isn't."

"Upstairs. On the right." Her head dropped back over his arm, the slender stalk of her neck pure and white.

He ran his lips down the smooth column of her throat, lingering in the hollow he found at its base, inhaling deeply. There was that "come hither" scent again, and abruptly his brain shut down and his body took over.

He had no conscious memory of carrying her up the stairs, although he must have. When he lifted his head and let her slide down to her feet, they were standing beside her bed. They both gasped at the fleeting caress over sensitized flesh as she slowly flowed over him. Reaching around her, he drew her shirt up and over her head, then tore at the waistband of her shorts, popping a button in his haste. Her body was beautiful; he wanted to stop and appreciate the small, pert breasts shielded beneath the pale pink bra, the flat belly that disappeared beneath the matching panties, the way her long, coltish legs met her torso, hiding her feminine flesh between them.

But he couldn't. He stripped away the panties and bra, leaving her body bared to his hot gaze. With a groan, he lifted her in his arms and set her on the bed. His fingers shook, but he managed to rip off his clothing in seconds, putting a knee on the mattress and coming down over her before her back hit the bed. He wedged a knee between her legs and opened a space for himself as his mouth took hers again in a deep, sure claiming, a precursor of his purpose. Her breath was rushing in and out. He kissed a path down the gentle swell of one breast and fastened his mouth on the pink-tipped crest, suckling strongly. She screamed and arched against him. He could feel the furious beat of his pulse echoed in the shaft between his legs as the soft curls at the junction of her thighs pushed at him. Frantically, he reared back and set his palms on the sleek muscles of her inner thighs, clearing the way for his invasion of the moist flesh that lay bared to him. A shift of his body positioned him at the entrance to her secrets, then his hips flexed, his buttocks clenched, and he drove forward in one stroke.

Frannie cried out sharply. She placed the palms of her hands against his shoulders as if to shove him away. As if she could.

Panting heavily, he stilled and looked down at her as shocked comprehension dawned. Her face was averted and the glorious body in which he nested—*God, she felt good!*—was stiff and drawn into an uncomfortable arch. Panic roared through him, and instinctively, he began to withdraw.

A whimper escaped her; her hands flew down to clench on his buttocks like talons. "Don't move. Please."

He froze, caught between the sweet pleasure of feeling her slick passage clasping him and the pain he could see he had given her. Hoarsely, he demanded, "Why didn't you tell me?"

"I...wasn't thinking." Her eyes met his, and in them he

read feminine vulnerability and a shy awareness that inflated a totally inappropriate bubble of possession inside him, given their current state.

"I wasn't thinking, either." He could say that with all honesty. He braced himself on his elbows and caught her face between his palms, forcing her to look at him. "If I'd known, I'd have gone about this differently." He grimaced. "A lot differently. How in the name of God does a thirty-two-year-old woman manage to stay a virgin in this day and age?"

He felt, rather than saw her shrug, and he realized the self-directed anger twisting in his gut must have shown in his voice.

"I told you I didn't have much time for normal dating when I was younger," she said with quiet dignity. "The opportunity never arose."

Thank God. A primitive surge of pleasure tore through him. No other man had ever known what it was like to lie between her long, lovely legs. No other man had known how tight and sweet the hot clasp of her lithe body felt around him, how swollen and red her lips were from his kisses as he took her.

He felt himself throb and pulse inside her, and suddenly he realized how desperately he needed her to enjoy what was happening between them. Dropping his head, he took her lips again in a gentle kiss that enticed and entreated, persuading her to relax the rigid set of her body. He nibbled his way along her jaw to her ear and felt her shiver of response. His body shouted at him to get moving, to hurry and begin the rhythmic dance toward fulfillment, but he held himself still with ruthless control. "I'm sorry," he breathed. "Do you want me to stop?"

He sure as hell hoped she wasn't going to say yes, because he didn't know if he could bring himself to leave unfinished what he'd started. But if she asked him to stop, he'd stop.

And pack ice in his briefs for the rest of the night.

She turned her head slightly as he continued to feather kisses along her temple, to nuzzle that special place where the smell of her gathered, and he realized that she was angling her neck to give him better access. "Don't stop," she said. "Just go slowly."

He almost laughed aloud, but he was afraid he might break down and howl like Lex at her most frustrated. Did she have any idea what she was asking?

No. Of course not. How could she?

Leaning slightly to one side, he drew a hand over the ridges of her ribs, marveling at how silky her skin was. A short detour led to her breast, where the silkiness was underlaid by the soft tissue that proclaimed her sex. He brushed a thumb over the nipple, and she made a small humming noise deep in her throat as the flesh drew into a taut bud. His own rigid flesh leaped in response, and to his grateful surprise, she lifted her hips the merest bit, pushing him deeper.

"You feel good in me," she whispered.

Damn the woman! She couldn't be any more arousing if she'd had years of practice at pleasing him. "I couldn't have said it better," he answered, and it was little more than a growl.

She moved against him again, definitely wriggling this time. "It doesn't hurt anymore," she announced. "It feels...like I'm waiting for something."

"You are," he assured her. He dared to withdraw halfway from her heated depths, and slowly filled her again. "Let me show you." He slipped a hand down between their bodies and teased the small nubbin he found above the site of their union. He rotated his finger once, massaging gently.

Her heels dug into the bed and her body thudded against him; he heard her gasp. He touched her with a bolder stroke, and the gasp became a sob. Her hips began to rock beneath him, creating an irresistible friction around him until he couldn't wait any longer. Withdrawing his hand, he gripped her hips and began a steady driving rhythm that matched her movements. He knew she wasn't with him, that she wasn't going to find out what she was waiting for just yet, but he had no control; his body was calling the shots. Within seconds he felt the forerunners of his climax stretching and stiffening him to unbearable proportions; he braced himself over her on his forearms and gave in to the desperate race, pounding against her again and again until, shaking like an oak in a hurricane, his hips plunged once, twice and his seed spilled into her as he shuddered and jerked in her arms.

Spent, he collapsed on her, his face buried in the silk of her hair. His chest heaved, and he fought for air, for control. He knew he was too heavy for her; in a moment he'd move. But right now his limbs felt like his bones were made of cement blocks. He couldn't lift an arm if he tried.

Her arms were around his back as far they could reach; she used her fingernails to lightly scratch up and down, over and over again as his heart rate slowed and his breath stopped hitching with every inhalation. The sensation was so intensely pleasurable that he couldn't prevent the contented groan that escaped him. A last, involuntary shiver slithered down his spine, and he felt his satisfied flesh twitch once more in its snug bed.

Her hips lifted against him.

A sudden flash of understanding brought comprehension. He'd forgotten her. He knew that he hadn't been able to wait, that he'd finished satisfying his own desperate need without giving her the same pleasure, and he recognized her restless movement...recognized it and was all too willing to help her find what she was seeking.

Lifting himself away from her, he slipped to one side. The loss of warmth chilled him as he withdrew from her; from the little whimper she made, he could tell she didn't like it, either. He placed one big hand flat on her belly and looked down into her face.

Her pretty, wide mouth with its pouty lower lip was still,

her big doe eyes serious. He bent and dropped a kiss on her brow, then another on the tilt of her nose.

"Thank you," she said.

"For what?" Why was she thanking him? As far as he was concerned, she'd given him an irreplaceable gift.

She placed her hand atop his, then lightly ran it up his arm. "I always wondered what the big fuss was about sex. Then I met you and I could see why women get themselves into trouble with the wrong men. It really is a basic drive, isn't it?"

"Only with the right person," he said. "And I'm pretty damn glad you didn't find him before."

She giggled. "I just bet."

His palm slipped up over the slight depression of her navel, over her rib cage, and farther until he'd covered a breast. He stimulated the still-tight peak with small circles and was pleased when her breath caught in her throat. "We didn't finish this," he told her.

Her eyes grew even wider. "We didn't?"

"No." Gathering both her hands in one of his, he anchored them above her head. "Now I get to show you what the big fuss is really about."

Her voice was nervous as she said, "Jack, I enjoyed it, too. Honestly. You don't have to— Oh!"

He was suckling at her breast, working the nipple and stroking it with his tongue, and again her hips arched involuntarily. "Do you like that?" he murmured against her skin.

"I—yes." It was a breath of sound.

"How about this?" He smoothed his free hand down over her belly again until his fingers just brushed the dark thatch of curls between her legs. Idly he caressed the soft flesh there.

She whispered, "Yes."

"And this?" His hand moved down to clasp her sex in his palm. Cupping her, he used the fleshy pad at the base of his thumb to press and stroke the spot he knew was waiting for his touch.

She whimpered, arching again and pressing herself against his hand.

It was answer enough. He increased his rhythm, and her hips began to move in a rising, falling circular pattern that mimicked his pace. His mouth continued to pluck and suck at her breast, and she thrust her hips up at him. Without breaking stride, he slipped one stealthy finger into the sweet heart of her, reveling in the slippery heat he found. She cried out, and he lifted his head then, unwilling to miss seeing her face, needing to be sure he wasn't hurting her newly initiated flesh.

She had her eyes closed, head thrown back, neck straining. Her hands pulled against his restraining grip.

"Look at me," he commanded.

She opened her eyes, and in the brown depths he read a wild need, a desperate quest for release. Satisfaction surged through him and he pressed his captured finger upward against the sensitive wall of her womb, pushing her toward the edge.

Her eyes were locked on his. Her hands curled into tight fists and her heels lifted her off the bed. Her breath began to rush in and out in a frantic, uncoordinated gasping and her body shuddered and bucked beneath his hand. He could feel her sweet internal muscles contracting again and again, and he realized he was as hard and ready as if he hadn't just taken her mere minutes ago.

The motion of her hip against him urged him to thrust strongly against her, but as her body quieted, he forced himself to halt. She'd been a virgin thirty minutes before; just because he was ready for round two didn't mean he should take advantage of her.

Her eyelids slipped down to shield her thoughts from him as he slipped his hand from her and bent to take her mouth briefly. "Now do you get it?"

Her lips curved up into a sweet smile. "Now I get it."

There was nothing he wanted more than to continue their intimate games, but conscience brought back memory. "I'd better go check on Lex," he said.

He rolled and rose from the bed, then padded down the stairs naked. Alexa was sleeping the sleep of the truly innocent, and he grinned as he gathered her into one arm and hefted the portable crib in the other. She could sleep just as easily here as she could at home in her own bed.

His eyes had adjusted to the dark, and he needed no light as he settled the crib in a room just across the hall from Frannie's bedroom and laid the infant down again without even waking her. Then he returned to his woman.

She was lying right where he'd left her, and he knew a surprising sense of pleasure that she hadn't jumped up to dress right away. Pulling back the covers, he slipped in beside her and curled around her, like two spoons nestled in a drawer. With a sigh, she twisted her head around and kissed his chin, then let herself go limp.

He glanced at the clock. "It's silly to leave now. I'll let Lex sleep and go get a change of clothes in the morning." Then he pulled her more closely back against him, savoring the press of his hips into the crease of her buttocks. He jumped as he felt her reach back and touch him, and his flesh leaped beneath her hand.

"Jack?" she whispered. "Do you want to…?"

He chuckled. "Can't you tell?" But he pulled her hand away and laid it against his hip. "But you'll be too sore. We'll take it easy until you're a little more used to this."

He felt her huff out a breath of what sounded like indignation, then a groan welled up in his throat as she deliberately rubbed her bottom back and forth against him. He felt himself immediately grow as stiff as a flagpole again.

"What if I don't want to take it easy?" There was the merest thread of laughter in her whisper this time.

He gritted his teeth. God save him from a woman who

was using him to test her newfound sexual powers. "Go to
sleep," he said, and there was more than a hint of steel in
his voice as he tucked her head beneath his chin on the
pillow.

Seven

One of the twins was fussing.

Frannie fought to swim to the surface of dreamless sleep. She was warm. Incredibly cosy, in fact. She struggled to sit up, but the movement was hampered by a heavy weight.

A groan in her ear brought memory flooding back.

Jack was here. With her. And last night he'd made love to her in a shattering, earth-shaking experience that she knew she would recall and cherish for the rest of her life. She'd never imagined that the act of accepting a man into your body could be so much more than…simply physical. And in her heart she recognized that sex always would be only sex unless she was making love with Jack.

A wave of revulsion, all the stronger for being unexpected, swept across her at the mere idea of another man touching her the way Jack had.

His arm was the weight she'd felt, and it lifted as he rolled away from her onto his back and then heaved himself into a sitting position. The child's discontent began to el-

evate into outright aggravation and she realized it was
Alexa making the noise.

"I'm coming, I'm coming," Jack muttered as he tossed
back the covers and rolled to his feet, stark naked and apparently not nearly as aware of it as she. He started for the
door, then stopped, pivoted and walked back to her side.
In one swift motion he bent, lifted her into his arms and
set his mouth on hers, kissing her with an expert thorough-
ness that made her toes curl and her arms come up to clutch
at his muscled shoulders. When she was hanging limp and
breathless in his embrace, he lifted his head and flashed her
that self-assured, cocky grin. This morning, though, it held
an element of intimacy, something just between them.
"Good morning."

Then he set her back on the bed, turned and strode out
of the room.

"Holy cow." She lay where he had left her for a minute.
Being handled as if she weighed no more than Alexa would
take some getting used to. In her mind's eye, she saw his
furred chest, bulging biceps, flat belly…and the heavy male
sex cushioned in the curling hair at his groin. The only
naked men she'd ever seen were her brothers when they
were small, and her nephews, so she had nothing to judge
by. Jack was a big man. It followed, didn't it, that he would
be…big, all over? Still, she doubted that every man in the
world was so well proportioned.

She shifted her weight to her side and swung her legs to
the floor as she sat up. Her body didn't feel any different,
except for the slightest tenderness between her legs. Unbelievable. She felt as though her entire life had been altered by last night; her body should give some sign of it.

Alexa's crying had stopped. She glanced at the clock,
realizing that it was Wednesday, and that April came in at
eight. She'd better warn Jack, or both he and her assistant
could get quite a surprise. She grinned as she decided that
April wouldn't mind a surprise like that one little bit.

But *she* would. She had never considered herself a jealous person, had had little call to experience the emotion, but she instinctively knew she wouldn't like it at all.

She put on a robe and went downstairs to make coffee, wondering if Jack ate a big breakfast. The answering machine was blinking when she passed it on the kitchen wall. How long had it been since she checked it? Not last night, that was for sure.

She punched the Replay button on the machine, and heard her own voice greeting the callers. Then her friend Jillian's voice filled the room. "Hey, Frannie, it's Jill. Got something for you to think about while you stitch. Dee needs to move, and she wants someplace that she can have her shop as well. Keep your ears to the ground and let her know if you hear of anything. Tomorrow's Wednesday, so I'll see you at noon. Farewell, sweetie."

"Is that Deirdre Patten she's talking about?"

The deep voice behind her made her jump, and she turned to face Jack, frowning over the message. "Yes," she said. "Her marriage fell apart last year but her ex is still hassling her. I imagine that house doesn't hold a lot of happy memories for her."

"Her brother told me her husband was screwing some woman he worked with."

The language might be a bit blunt, but she couldn't have said it better. "That's about right. Did he mention the jerk hasn't given her a penny to support his sons since he left?"

Jack's eyebrows came together. He rubbed his palm over his chin, then snapped his fingers. "I might know a place that would work for her. It's an old farmhouse on a couple of acres just up the road—gorgeous if you're into rustic and historical. The owner's desperate to sell and she probably could bargain." Then he frowned. "But I guess that wouldn't work. She needs someplace where her shop is highly visible."

"No, she doesn't. She makes designer doll clothes. Most of her business is special order by mail. It doesn't matter where she's located."

"Designer doll clothes? Only in the nineties." He nodded, as if making a mental note as he set Alexa in her baby seat and settled on a stool to drink his coffee. "I'll call the guy today and see how low I can get him to go on it."

"Thank you." She came around the end of the bar and put her arms around his neck. "I appreciate it." When he hooked his arms around her and drew her between his knees for a kiss, she lifted her face and pressed herself against him, opening her mouth and welcoming his tongue, loving the growing bulge against her stomach. He made a sound low in his throat and his arms tightened for a moment.

Then he grabbed her arms and set her away from him. "If we keep that up, I can tell you I'll never make it to the office today."

She smiled. "Would that be so bad?"

"At least I'd declare bankruptcy with a smile on my face." He rose from the stool and drained his coffee cup, one arm loosely around her shoulders. "I've got to get going. I'll see you later."

"All right."

He stopped and waited until she looked up at him. "Get rid of your little black book, baby. You have my brand stamped on your forehead now." Then he added, "I'll burn mine this morning."

Her mouth fell open, and he gently closed it with one finger, his gray eyes warm with humor. "I'll bring a change of clothes along tonight."

She gulped and nodded as he left the room and she heard the front door open and close. Relief unfurled within her. Beneath the happiness had been a fear that their lovemaking hadn't been the same extraordinary experience for him that it had been for her. His proprietary tone reassured her as nothing else could have. Whatever he felt for her, Jack wanted her and only her in his bed.

As she did him. Forever.

Alexa was wide-awake, watching her from her little seat propped on the counter.

"Your uncle's a charmer," Frannie informed her. "But I love him, anyway."

The morning went smoothly, despite Alexa's presence in the shop. It was fairly busy, with three final fittings and two potential clients who were planning weddings for the following winter. All of the women had brought friends or relatives along, and many of them drooled over Alexa, carrying her around and cooing at her.

After the fourth time someone told her she had a beautiful daughter, Frannie gave up trying to explain and simply said, "Thank you." If only this *were* her baby. The longing caught her flat-footed and she had to stop and take a deep breath. Where in the heck had that come from? Hadn't she had enough of babies in her life? Perhaps. But they hadn't been her own, and it was foolish to deny that little could make her happier than having children of her own someday. Unfortunately, the only man she could envision in that role was Jack, and she refused, absolutely refused, to allow herself to dream of that possibility. She would take each day she got and store the memories away because she knew it wouldn't last. Once he was firmly on his feet as a father, she'd be less important in his life. And even though he wanted her now, she could never hope to hold a man like Jack.

April went off to have lunch with her boyfriend at noon, and Frannie flipped the Open sign over to Closed behind her. She had just finished warming a bottle when the doorbell rang.

Juggling the baby and the bottle, she tossed a cloth diaper over her shoulder and opened the door one-handed.

Jillian stood on the stoop.

It was hard to say who was more surprised.

"Oh, no! It's Wednesday!" Frannie backed away from the door and motioned Jill in. They had a standing lunch date every week, and this week it had been scheduled for her shop. "I am so sorry. I completely forgot you were coming. I haven't prepared a thing." Then she glanced down at the baby. "Unless you like formula."

Jillian stepped inside and closed the door herself, then turned and gave Frannie a long, thorough inspection from under lowered brows. "What are you doing with that?" she said in a voice that clearly indicated Frannie was losing her faculties. "Did we or did we not have a long conversation about standing up to one's family when free babysitting was requested? Did we not swear that from now on we would see said family on our terms, and that we would not be at their beck and call?"

"She's not family." It was silly to feel so defensive, she told herself. "I'm doing a favor for a friend in exchange for some free advertising." Which wasn't exactly a lie, although it hadn't really transpired that way.

Jillian's expression lightened. "Good girl! You mean you aren't letting someone take gross and blatant advantage of your good nature?"

"No way. This is strictly a business arrangement." Liar, an inner voice taunted. She ignored it and forced herself to smile at her friend. "So come on in and we'll scrounge up something for lunch. How long do you have?"

Jillian checked the elegant little gold watch on her left wrist as they walked into the kitchen. "About an hour and a half. Marina owed me for yesterday, when she went to the doctor." She hesitated, looked down at the powder blue suit she wore, and muttered, "Oh, what the hell. I'm dying to hold that baby."

Frannie laughed. "Be my guest. You feed her, I'll find something to feed us." She handed Alexa to Jill and turned to check the contents of the fridge.

"Now this is the way to go if you want a baby," Jillian commented as she settled Alexa in one arm. "Borrow somebody else's and skip the pregnancy part altogether."

Pregnant! The thought stopped her cold. Good Lord, she'd never even thought about birth control until now!

"What's the matter?" Jill was looking at her curiously.

"Nothing." She forced herself to natural actions, sniffed the tuna salad—still good—and scooped rounded mounds of it onto the lettuce she'd arranged on two plates. Deliberately she set her concern in the back of her mind, to worry over when she was alone.

"This child is beautiful," Jill said softly, surprising Frannie. "What's her name?"

"Alexa." She'd never really imagined Jillian wanting much to do with children, but she couldn't have been more wrong, she thought, watching Jill's face as she rocked Alexa. The naked hunger in her expression squeezed Frannie's heart. Did Jill want children of her own someday? She didn't have the nerve to ask. They'd been fast friends from the day they'd met at a business seminar, but Frannie sensed there was a part of Jillian that was deeply reserved, private and hidden from the world. And there was a huge, unmistakable Keep Out sign posted across its entrance.

She finished setting the table, peeled some kiwi and oranges and divided the fruit between the two plates. Then she garnished the tuna salad with parsley and carried the plates to the table.

Alexa had finished eating, and Jill slung a cloth diaper over her shoulder before lifting her to her shoulder for a bubble. When Alexa let out a man-sized burp, she laughed and brought her down to nestle in one arm, waving Frannie away. "No, don't take her. I can eat with one hand." She proved it by picking up her fork and digging delicately into the tuna.

Frannie followed suit as she asked, "So what good dirt do you know that I don't?" It was a standard joke among the two of them and Dee. That led her to her next question. "Have you talked to Dee? I haven't talked to her since I saw her at a lacrosse game last week."

"You were at a lacrosse game?" The idea clearly intrigued Jill. Then a shadow crossed her expressive face. "Dee is Not Good. Very, very Not Good. In fact, she was in tears when I called her last night, so I went over. Nelson was there.''

Frannie sighed. ''That guy is lower than dirt. She should have divorced him years ago when he threw the first woman in her face.''

''I agree. But she wants so desperately to keep their relationship civil for the sake of the boys.... Did you know he left a threatening message on her answering machine?''

''You're kidding. That's scary.''

Jill nodded grimly. ''She finally agreed to press charges after I told her this is how women get killed. I gave the tape to the cops. They promised to pay him a visit and impress upon him that he will go to jail if he doesn't stay away from her.''

''Good.''

Her friend rose and handed Alexa to Frannie, then began to stalk around the room. ''I've never been big on vigilanteeism, but I'm rapidly changing my mind. For a minute there, I actually wished I owned a gun. Just to shoot out his tires,'' she added when she saw Frannie's shocked face.

''You can't just take the law into your own hands. However—'' Frannie held up a finger when Jillian's brows snapped together and she opened her mouth. ''If he ever lays a hand on her or the boys again, I promise you I'll be right beside you when we break his neck.''

A smile tugged at the corners of Jillian's fine features. ''That's the spirit.''

Frannie had always thought of her as a Norse goddess, with her flawless roses-and-cream complexion and her wide blue eyes that shouted out both intelligence and fierce independence. Her policy in regard to men had broken more than one heart. She told them up-front she was out for a good time, and if they got serious about her, it was their tough luck. And she wasn't kidding.

Now she said to Frannie, ''You're right. There's really nothing we can do for now.''

''Except be there when she needs us.''

Jill nodded. "Except be there." Her blue eyes were resigned. "One thing's for sure, she's got to get out of that house."

"Um, actually, I might have a lead on something."

Jill's face lit up. "Wow! Already?"

"Well, I had some help," Frannie admitted. "And it's only a possibility."

"So talk!"

"Jack—Jack Ferris—knows a place in the country with some land. He's checking on it this morning."

"It's like Jack to take on something like this," Jillian said, letting Alexa drag one of her fingers toward her mouth with the zeal of a great white shark on a binge. "He's a real sweetie, isn't he?"

Frannie couldn't help it. She knew she was blushing. Thank heavens Jill was playing with the baby. Quickly she turned away, folding a length of fabric and storing it back in its place on the wall before turning around. "Yes. He's nice." There, that was a neutral answer.

Unfortunately Jillian had a ear for discerning any prevarication. She eyed Frannie speculatively. "You already spoke to Jack this morning? That was fast."

Heat was creeping up her cheeks, and she knew it showed in her face. She couldn't lie, but she wasn't ready to share the details of her relationship with Jack yet. Not until she knew them herself.

Jillian was laughing now. "I'm beginning to get the picture." Suddenly her eyes sharpened and she looked at Alexa more closely. "Just whose baby is this that you're keeping in exchange for advertising?"

"Jack's," she admitted.

"Jack's? Since when did Jack Ferris become a father? Who's the mother?"

So she was forced to explain the whole story. Almost. She neglected to mention the tiny matter of Jack's sleeping arrangements last night, and she prayed that Jillian couldn't see the truth in her face. Jack had said he'd branded her forehead; she was afraid maybe it was less of a jest than he'd intended.

Jill wore a troubled expression when she finished, and Frannie had a feeling she wasn't thinking of Alexa's orphaned status. "Be careful, sweetie, please? Jack makes women feel gorgeous and special with just one look from those eyes. But he doesn't really mean it personally. It's just his way. Don't take on this responsibility hoping it's going to lead to something more. I knew his wife." She made a moue of distaste as she went on. "And I can guarantee you she ruined him for life."

"I'm only helping him until he finds a permanent placement that we—he thinks is right for Alexa." But it sounded weak, even to her own ears.

"Well, I've delivered my motherly lecture," Jillian said, making a show of dusting off her hands as she came to hug Frannie, though concern still lurked in her pretty eyes. "Enough with the advice. I have to get moving. Wait until I tell my sister I spent my lunch hour feeding Jack Ferris's baby!"

Jack walked in the door at five-thirty that evening. He didn't knock; he just walked in as if he'd lived there all his life.

She was in the kitchen chopping fresh carrots to put in with a pot roast she intended to cook the next day. When she looked up and saw him in the doorway, sheer unadulterated joy ripped her composure to shreds. But even as he started forward, she schooled herself to act casually. The mere sight of him made her stomach clench and her breath come faster. One day, these moments would come to an end and she didn't want Jack to walk away thinking he'd broken her heart.

Then he was beside her, reaching for her, and all coherent thought fled.

Their evening was much the same as the one before. He carried her up to her bedroom as soon as Alexa was down for the night and loved every inch of her with urgent caresses. The chief difference was that tonight, he held himself back until he'd brought her to a frantic, sobbing climax before he allowed himself release within her body. When he rolled from her, he immediately curled around her as he had the night before, kissed her ear and was asleep with the suddenness of a light winking off. She wanted to stay awake, to savor the sweetness of the moment and the embrace, but his total relaxation affected her, as well, and she fell asleep in the cradle of his arms.

In the middle of the night, she awakened again to find he'd already turned her to her back and soon he was moving inside her, his hard length stoking the embers of desire within her to a roaring blaze that he patiently fed until finally she flew apart beneath him, burning so hot that she engulfed him, sending him rocketing into his own fierce finish. Afterward, he simply gathered her against him again and she fell back to sleep with his breath playing over her neck and his hand cradling her breast in silent possession.

And Friday was the same. Later that night, when she thought he was asleep, his voice growled in the darkness, "I wish you were coming with me tomorrow." He meant the charity tournament Stu had roped him into, and she was pleased all out of proportion to the simple statement. He wanted her with him!

Aloud, all she said was, "I promised to baby-sit a long time ago."

He was silent then, and she thought that was the end of the discussion. Then he said, "I'll drive you out in the morning."

She was startled and she half turned in the darkness to face him. "That's silly. It would take you more than an hour round-trip." Then it occurred to her that he might be worrying about his niece's safety, so she said, "I'm a careful driver. Alexa will be safe with me."

He chuckled and his voice was warm with amusement in the intimate cocoon of midnight that surrounded them. "My motives are purely selfish. If I take you, then I have to come back and pick you up. Nothing is going to keep you from coming home to me for even one night."

That shook her so completely that her mind went blank. By the time she realized she should say something, so much time had elapsed that anything would sound strange. So she remained silent, but she rolled fully into his arms so that her body was aligned with his, throwing her leg over his and wrapping her arms around him. He rolled onto his back, taking her with him and settling her on his chest so that the steady sound of his heartbeat lulled her to sleep with her limbs still twined around him.

On Saturday morning, they overslept. Frannie hadn't set an alarm, since Alexa was always hungry around 6:00 a.m. It figured that she would decide to stretch her night's sleep to nearly eight.

Frannie woke first, raising her head from Jack's chest to check the clock face when she realized the room was lighter than it should be. "Holy cow!" She leaped off him, covers flying. Had something happened to Alexa in the night?

"What's wrong?" Jack bolted out of bed from a sound sleep, shaking his head to clear it.

"I have to check the baby." She left the room at a run. She never slept this late. Had she stopped breathing? Smothered in the blanket?

After a glance at the clock, he ran after her. Frannie reached the crib an instant before he did—

—and stopped dead. Jack skidded to a halt right behind her.

"She's fine." She gazed at the baby, who had started to stretch and squirm from her sleep when she heard voices. Adrenaline was still rushing through her veins, and she put one hand on the crib rail for support, the other over her heaving breast. "Thank God she's all right."

"I can't believe she slept this long. That's over nine hours." Jack's voice was awed.

She had regained some of her composure and she looked over her shoulder at him. "I'm sorry if I scared you. I just had this horrible fear that something had happened—"

"I know." He reached around her and set his hands on the rail, too, enclosing her within the circle formed by his arms as he dropped a kiss to the top of her bare shoulder. "I flipped, too, when I saw what time it was." He looked down at his niece. "Good morning, princess. I bet you'll be ready for action today."

They both laughed when a beatific smile spread over the baby's face and she squealed in a distinct effort to greet them.

His chest pressed against her back as they both leaned over the crib, and she realized that they were both stark naked. Sheepishly she said, "I hope seeing us like this won't scar her for life."

Jack laughed. "In about two minutes, she's going to get hungry. She'll have forgotten all about us." Then he stiffened behind her. "Oh, man, tell me it isn't really eight o'clock."

Simultaneously they straightened and looked at each other. "We're late!"

As it turned out, they just made it. After thirty minutes of rushing around dressing and gathering up baby supplies before driving off, they pulled into the driveway of her family home at exactly the time she'd promised to arrive. Jack would still make the tournament if he didn't linger when he dropped her off.

None of her brothers were in sight as he carried Alexa in her portable infant seat to the front porch and set her down. "I can't stay right now, but when I come back, I want to meet your family."

"All right. I hope the tournament's a success." She looked up at him and couldn't prevent herself from smoothing her palm over the shoulder of his uniform, loving the solid feel of the muscle beneath. Then she thought of the sport in which he was about to participate, and the sound of bodies hitting the ground came all too clearly. "Be careful."

"Don't worry." He took her by the waist and pulled her against him. "You're my battery pack. This will keep me

going when my energy's just a memory." Then his arms
went around her, and as his mouth came down, she met
him eagerly, straining against him with all the love she
couldn't voice, until he reluctantly broke the kiss. "If you
don't walk up those steps right now, we're liable to give
your family a biology lesson."

She smiled, scratching her nails up and down his back
in the manner he loved, making him arch like a big cat
under her hands. "Is that so?"

"That's so." He pressed a final, hard kiss to her lips and
stepped back. "Think of me today."

"Aye-aye, cap'n." She saluted him with her right hand
and smiled brilliantly as he turned away, keeping the smile
pinned on until his newly purchased van rolled down the
driveway. As the sound of the engine faded, so did her
smile, until she briskly shook herself and reached for the
handle of the infant carrier. She was not going to moon
over the man all day like some lovesick cow.

Behind her the front door opened.

"Was the guy you were just peeling yourself away from
the same guy who answered your phone when Robert
called the other night?" Her brother Donald didn't sound
as if he was very happy. Oh, well, he'd never been a morning person.

"It was," she answered levelly. "His name is Jack Ferris."

"And when do we get to meet him?" Donald was taller
than she, but she'd taken care of him for too many years
to be intimidated when he stepped forward.

"He'll be back to pick me up this evening. And—" she
poked a stiff finger into her brother's chest "—you will be
polite to him, young man."

Donald held the threatening posture for a long moment.
Then his lips twitched. As they both burst out laughing, he
reached out to hug her. "Ah, Frannie, we really miss you."

Eight

When the van crunched to a halt in the driveway of Frannie's brother's house that evening, Jack took his time releasing his seat belt and getting out of the van. Part of the reason was his left knee, on which he'd held ice the whole way out here to try to limit the spread of the enormous bruise that was slowly, inexorably forming. The other part was curiosity. Frannie had grown up in this house; he wanted to be able to picture her here.

In counterpoint, a little voice in his head was telling him to move, to get inside the house and find his woman. He was doing his best to ignore it.

Driving away earlier in the day, he'd had the weirdest feeling…he didn't want to play lacrosse, didn't want to spend his Saturday hanging out with his teammates at a nearby watering hole between games. He wanted to be with Frannie and Alexa.

He had told himself he was pathetic. Peer pressure was getting to him. Just because almost all of his pals went home to warm-bodied wives and lively, bouncing little ones at the end of the day didn't mean he had to.

Just because the guys spent half their bench time discussing pediatricians and preschools didn't mean he had to. So what if he'd happened to mention his day care dilemma and Quentin Jernigan had said he'd check his son's day care and see if they had any openings in the infant room coming up soon.

Just because Slick Wetzall had had his four-month-old daughter at the game, showing her off to anybody who would look, didn't mean he had to. And just because he'd held Slick's little kid until someone else protested that he was hogging the baby didn't mean he wanted a pack of his own.

When he'd realized Stu had more than enough players to make up a team, he'd forced himself not to hop in his new, family-oriented van and hightail it back out to Taneytown. So he'd stayed, playing half-assed lacrosse and counting the hours till the tournament's end. Just because he couldn't concentrate on another damned thing except those sweet little noises Frannie made when he pushed himself into the warm center of her didn't mean he was letting himself think of her too much.

He refused to be ruled by any part of his body other than his brain.

But that's just what had been happening, he assured himself. Great sex was a rarity. Having it with someone you liked and enjoyed being with was a definite bonus. So how come, when Wendy Marshall, with whom he'd spent a few totally incredible nights during the bad days after Lannette left, had walked by and winked familiarly at him, he hadn't had the slightest desire to chase her down and renew old ties?

Compatibility. That's all it was. He and Frannie could talk, something he'd never known with Wendy. Or Lannette either, for that matter. He'd spent so much of his time with Lannette simply trying to be with her that he'd never noticed it before.

He decided that being with Frannie, with her warmth, her sense of humor and her practical streak, was infinitely preferable to the Wendys of the world. And, if he was honest, far better than being with his wife had ever been.

From there, it was an easy leap to the next decision.

He would marry Frannie.

Once he'd sworn he would never get trapped in matrimony again, but this was different. He might not love her, but he liked her, which was far more important. Frannie was his friend as well as the woman who had writhed beneath him in passion a few hours ago. As his body recalled just exactly how enthusiastically she had writhed, the jock-strap he wore beneath his uniform shorts became a prison, and he adjusted himself to relieve the pressure a bit. Better not think about that part of their relationship. Instead, he'd better consider the best way to get Frannie to agree to marry him.

She didn't have that hungry, hunting look that so many unattached women did, that yes-I'll-marry-you-tomorrow attitude. She had never mentioned any permanence between them. He had, and it hadn't escaped him that she'd made no comment whatsoever. In fact, she seemed to take a mental step back, retreat into herself, whenever he pushed too hard. And the harder he pushed, the more remote she became. Last night, when he'd blurted out that stupid comment about wishing she were coming to the tournament, her whole body had stiffened in his arms for a second, though all she'd done was remind him that she'd made this other commitment.

As he limped toward the little ranch house with its light brick and faded, yellow paint, the same color that decorated the small stable set at the back of the lot, the way to get Frannie to agree to wear his ring came to him.

Court her. That's what he'd have to do. Tricky, certainly, with Lex as his permanent sidekick, but definitely doable.

Yep, he'd court her, make her feel special, let her see how good a union between them could be for both of them as well as Lex. He didn't love her, didn't want to spend every waking minute with her, so he'd never be in the same position he'd been in with Lannette.

Never again. But he could make her feel special, because she would be.

The front door flew open just as he began to mount the three steps, and Frannie appeared. As she hurried down the steps and wedged herself under his arm as a living crutch—which felt damn good, both for his knee and for the rest of him—she demanded, "What in the world happened?"

"Yeah, I missed you, too," he said wryly.

She stopped dead, slanting a sudden smile his way. "I'm glad you're back."

He supposed it could have been worse. But it sure as hell could have been better.

He'd made a pest of himself once, simply by wanting to share his whole life with his wife. And what had happened? She'd accused him of making her feel like a Siamese twin, of never giving her any "space," whatever the hell that meant.

Then Frannie stepped in front of him, lightly placed her hand against his chest for balance and lifted herself on tip-toe to give him a gentle kiss, and he forgot everything but the feel of her soft mouth welcoming him.

"There," she said, and her eyes were dancing. "Is that better?"

"A little." He put his hand to her head, threading his big, rough fingers through the fine silk of her dark hair to cradle her skull. Holding her in place, he returned the kiss—his way. Harder, deeper, hotter, until she was making that little purring sound that turned him on even more. "That's better," he said, releasing her.

The sound of a throat clearing with an ostentatious cough startled them both. Looking over Frannie's head, he checked out the man standing in the doorway. He was a good bit younger than himself, Jack figured, and not nearly as big, though he had to be close to six foot. And he looked exactly like Frannie. Or as close as a man could look, given the addition of whiskers and the absence of a dash of makeup.

Meeting a man whose sister had just given you the extra leg in your pants wasn't exactly an auspicious start, but he guessed there was no help for it.

Mounting the final step, Jack stuck out his hand. It was always good to take an offensive posture. "Jack Ferris. Nice to meet you."

The guy stepped up and took the offered hand, and for a moment they did the ritual familiar only to men who judged one another on the basis of a firm handshake. When Jack finally squeezed the bones of the younger man's hand just enough to hurt a teeny bit, the guy relaxed his grip first. An important victory. "I'm Donald Brooks, Frannie's brother. Come on in. What happened to the knee?"

"A freight train." When Frannie and Donald both cast him identical, uncomprehending glances, he explained. "I made the stupid mistake of turning my head away from the defenseman in front of me for a minute too long. Got royally slammed. I think my knee might have been the first part of me to hit the ground."

Frannie winced. "I don't want to hear this."

They showed him into a modest living room decorated in navy and mauve, and he eased into a chair. Frannie propped his injured leg on a hassock and zipped off to get ice and check on Alexa, who was napping, she said.

Donald leaned back in a chair across from him and crossed his arms. "So," he said, "what do you do?"

"Advertising," Jack said easily. "That's how Frannie and I met."

"What happened to your wife?"

Jack raised an eyebrow. "She left me." It was way out of line, but he was determined not to pick a fight with Frannie's brother.

"She left you with a baby that young?" Donald's expression was scandalized. "Why?"

He couldn't help it. The laughter had to dribble out or he'd burst. "My wife left a long time ago. I don't have any kids," he explained, chuckling as Donald's expression turned to chagrin at his assumptions. "The baby is my niece." He felt the amusement flee and sorrow step into its place. "My brother and his wife were killed in an accident right after she was born."

Frannie had come back into the room with a towel and the ice pack during the last part. She leveled a warning look at her brother. "Stop it, Donald." To Jack, she said, "I apologize in advance for anything he might say. He thinks he's my protector. If he doesn't approve of you, it's a duel at dawn with water pistols."

Donald grinned, and Jack decided that under the right circumstances, Frannie's brother could be an okay kind of guy. To his sister, Donald said, "Somebody has to look out for you, sister, dear. After the last fiasco, I'm vetting all your dates."

Jack could tell the moment Donald uttered the words that he regretted them. An awkward silence fell. Frannie didn't reply, but Jack could have sworn her lip trembled for an instant. And in that instant he sensed that here was the information he needed to figure out what made her tick. He wasn't leaving this house tonight until he had that secret.

Donald rose from his chair. "Jeez, I'm sorry, Frannie. I didn't mean that the way it sounded." He clunked himself in the forehead with his fist. "Billy's right. I'm a dope even when I don't work at it."

"But sometimes you're definitely a bigger dope than others." It was a new voice, wry and clearly affectionate, and they all turned toward the speaker. Lounging in the kitchen entry was a boy—young man—Jack figured was probably about college age. His dark hair was long enough to pull back in a stubby ponytail, and an earring glinted from one ear. "Your wife wants you to start the grill when you're done being a doofus,'' he informed Donald. Then he walked across the room to Jack's chair and shook his hand. ''Hi, I'm Billy.''

Jack noticed there was none of the macho stuff in this handshake. Billy clearly regarded him as the dominant male in the room. It made sense. Jack figured anybody who ran around in shorts big enough for two people and worn with the crotch dragging halfway to his knees would have a hell of a time convincing anybody of his machoness.

Frannie made introductions while Donald quietly disappeared. Billy was her youngest brother, and it quickly became apparent that he was the broadcaster of the family chronicles. Without being asked.

He told Jack he was currently studying business management at the University of Maryland. In between Donald and Billy came Robert-of-the-phone-call, who was on a minivacation with his wife for the weekend, leaving their three kids with Donald and his wife. Which was why, Billy went on, they had called on Frannie today when one of their kids had a doctor's appointment scheduled....

Frannie interrupted Billy's ramblings. ''So when did the earring join your wardrobe?'' she asked.

Billy grinned. ''Now, now, Maw,'' he said. ''I'm a big boy, remember? I got the ear pierced about three weeks ago. I was going to ask if you like it, but I suspect I already know the answer.''

''I suspect you do.'' Frannie walked across the room and hugged her little brother, who topped her willowy height by several inches. ''But I still love you.''

Billy stuck a finger into her ribs, which made her scream and leap away. ''Actually, I'm thinking about a nose ring. Or maybe one in my belly button.''

''Right.'' She prudently kept a chair between her ribs and Billy's tickling fingers. ''I can't believe you even got the earring without someone holding you down. I know you and pain, remember? The guy who fainted when they drew blood for your high school physical?'' She turned to Jack with a wide smile. "I got this call from the school office that I had to come get him—"

"All right, all right. He gets the picture."

From the back of the house, a woman's voice called, "Frannie? Could you help me out with D.J., please? Bring your fella along so I can get a look at him."

Frannie grimaced as she turned toward the doorway. "That's Donald's wife. I'll introduce you in a little while. Want to sit and rest for a few minutes? I'll let you know when the burgers and 'dogs are ready."

No, he didn't want to sit and rest. He wanted to take Frannie into an empty room and strip off her clothes and kiss every inch of her long, pretty body, starting with the gentle curve of her buttocks barely hidden beneath the soft fabric of her white shorts. Since that didn't seem to be an option, he figured he'd sit tight and relax.

When she left the room, Billy took the seat Donald had just vacated. "So how long have you been seeing my sister?" he asked. If he hadn't been so openly friendly, Jack would have thought he was going to get another grilling.

"Not long enough," he replied. "But I hope I'll have plenty of time to remedy that."

Billy regarded him thoughtfully. "Wow. You mean, like, become part of the family?"

Jack shrugged. "You never know". And that was enough answering her brothers' snoopy questions. "I understand Frannie pretty much raised you and your brothers."

"There's no 'pretty much' about it," Billy informed him. "I don't even remember my mother. I was only two when she died. If Dad had remarried, Frannie might have had more time for herself. But he didn't, and then he died the year she graduated. And the four of us were so spread out in age that she was twenty-seven before I graduated from high school."

"But she had finished college by then." No question

about it, it was more fun to be the snoop*er* than the snoop*ee*.

"Nope. She went part-time for a long time until she got a two-year degree, but it wasn't until she finally decided to ditch the nursemaid role that she went back full-time and got a degree in clothing design." Billy was an absolute fountain of information, easily primed for maximum flow.

"You mean until you were grown."

"Not hardly. I mean after she finally realized she was spending her whole life taking care of other people's kids. It was an interesting day around this ol' homestead when she told Donald and Robert to start hunting for a sitter, 'cuz she was outta here." He shook his head and the earring—which Jack would die before he'd ever wear—glinted in a ray of late-afternoon sun that fell across his chair. "Those two dirt balls really took advantage of her."

"So let me get this straight," Jack said. "Frannie stayed at home after your dad died until you graduated. And then…?"

"And then when she finally got me out of her hair, Donald's first son was born with cerebral palsy and she helped take care of him. He started in a special preschool when he was two, but then Robert's wife had the twins and was in bed on doctor's orders for a few months, so Frannie helped them out, too."

"So what made her decide—"

"Billy?" Frannie's voice called from the rear of the home.

That was the end of Snoop Time, Jack realized regretfully.

"It's time to eat. Will you help Jack out to the table, please?"

Jack didn't really think he needed help, and apparently Billy didn't, either, because he waited at a respectful distance until Jack hauled himself to his feet on his one good leg. Then he showed him through the kitchen to the screened-in back porch, where a picnic-style supper had been set.

The first thing he noticed were the twins. Adorable little dark-haired girls who looked enough like their Aunt Frannie to be her own. They giggled and batted their eyes at him, and he was enchanted. This was what their babies would look like. His and Frannie's. He didn't want Lex to be an only child, and Frannie was so good with kids that she'd probably want a bunch. The idea tickled him.

The thought of children caused him to look around for his own kid. Frannie held her in one arm. With the other, she was patiently offering bits of food from a plate for a little boy in a wheelchair.

"They usually get him started early because it takes him longer," Billy said in an undertone from behind him.

Jack was stunned. The child looked as if he were easily five or six, and he was as helpless as a baby. He turned back toward Billy. "I thought people with cerebral palsy could walk with braces or walkers."

Billy snorted. "You're thinking of the poster child stuff. This is more often the real thing. His motor skills are pretty limited, but his mind is as sharp as yours and mine. They're teaching him to use a keyboard to help communicate because he's kind of hard to understand." His tone changed, became meaningful. "He's a great kid. We all love him."

And *you'd* better, too, was the unspoken message. It wasn't a problem, Jack decided, just a bit of a shock. Frannie hadn't told him much about her family; he could see now that she'd been the rock for them all during the years she normally would have been going to college, meeting guys, marrying and starting her own family. Suddenly her single state—and her unexpected virginity—began to make more sense.

Her sister-in-law was an attractive blonde who looked a bit ragged around the edges. "This is why I only have two kids," she said darkly, watching the twins and two other kids dropping more food on the floor than in their mouths and giggling like crazy when a fuzzy brown dog raced to gulp down the tidbits.

She directed him to the table, where Donald was setting down a tray of hot dogs and hamburgers, and he made himself a plate. Then it occurred to him that Frannie hadn't eaten yet, either. He waved at her across the porch, and when she looked over, indicated the table. "'Dog or burger?"

"Burger, please," she said, and the look on her face made him glad he'd thought about her. It was a little thing, but she appeared stunned that he would think to ask. He filled her plate with a little of everything, then limped over to sit next to her. Setting down the plates, he took Lex from her. She grinned and drooled and waved her little fists as if she recognized him, and his heart gave a little squeeze of pleasure. When he looked up, Frannie was watching him. On her face was a tender expression that he would pay a million bucks to see every day, and without thinking, he raised her hand to his lips and kissed it, keeping his eyes on hers until she looked away, over at her nephew sitting patiently in his wheelchair.

She patted the little boy's limp hand, which was drawn into an odd, taut curl. "I'd like you to meet my friend, Mr. Ferris."

"Just call me Uncle Jack," he said.

Uncle Jack. As Frannie bathed a screaming Alexa, who was at the end of her rope after such a big day, she thought about what Jack had said. Donald had nearly dropped an entire plate of raw hamburgers on the ground.

He hadn't meant it in any serious context, she was sure. Jack was just that way—genial and friendly, leaving new members of the Ferris Fan Club behind him wherever he went. Her family had certainly been taken with him. Especially her sister-in-law, whom she'd noticed sucking in her tummy and wiping mascara from beneath her eyes with a napkin when she thought nobody was looking.

Uncle Jack. She'd made him put yet another ice pack on his knee while she got Alexa ready for bed. She'd refused to let him drive home, and she'd had to bribe him with the TV clicker to keep him off his feet. So he currently was propped on her bed watching the Orioles trounce the Yankees for a second time straight. She'd already mixed a bottle, which sat on the nightstand beside the bed, and she'd promised to bring Alexa in to him to feed as soon as she was bathed. With the ever-increasing shrieking ringing in her ears, she decided he had gotten the best end of that deal.

The bath finished, she quickly diapered and dressed the baby, brushed her damp hair up into a funny little curl atop her head, and carried her in to Jack. He reached for the infant, sighing happily when she was snuggled in his arms taking her evening feeding.

"I missed this today," he said. "What was my life like before I had her?"

That wasn't a topic she was particularly hot to discuss. "Sane," she said. "How's the knee?"

He considered the question for a moment, flexing the leg slightly and wincing. "Not too bad," he pronounced. "I was afraid I might have cracked the kneecap, but I think it's just bruised." With his free hand, he reached out and tugged her closer to the bed. "Come sit with me," he said. "You've had a busy day."

She couldn't resist. She crawled up on the bed and settled beside him, closing her eyes when he put his free arm around her and drew her close, so that he wouldn't see the flood of emotion in her eyes. This was what she'd waited for all her life…if this wonderful fantasy were real and this was her family, it would be perfect. She enjoyed her business, but the bald truth that she hadn't wanted to face was that she would be perfectly happy to be a wife and mother, to design gowns when time permitted. It wasn't fashionable in this age of independent women, but it was her.

Alexa's eyes had rolled back in her head, and her rosebud lips were slack around the bottle. Chuckling, Jack shifted her to his shoulder. "I do this to all the women."

She snorted. "Yeah, I've noticed how bored women are when you're around. Did you know everyone's nicknamed you, Jack the Flirt Ferris?"

"They have?" His voice was suddenly much quieter, much cooler than it had been a moment ago. His arm around her felt stiff and uncomfortable. "And is that what you think?"

Self-protection kicked in. She'd fallen once for a man who didn't love her. At least this time she didn't have to let him know she was hurting. "What I think is beside the point."

"I see." He took his arm from around her and rose so suddenly that she nearly fell over. When he stifled a groan, she knew his knee must be terribly sore.

"I'll put her down," she offered. "You shouldn't be on that leg."

"She's my baby. I'll do it." He hobbled from the room, and she heard him stump across the hall. After a long moment he came limping back. He walked to the dresser and placed both hands on it with his back to her, leaning heavily.

She hadn't meant to hurt him, hadn't known he could be hurt. Remorse overcame her desire to safeguard her heart. She began to try to tell him so. "Jack, I never meant—"

"Dammit, woman!" he roared.

She jumped a foot in the air. She'd never heard him raise his voice before.

"You tell me I'm a flirt, you tell me everybody knows it, and you pretty much say straight up that it doesn't matter to you? *How in the hell do you think that makes me feel?*" He waved his hands in the air in short, chopped motions that told her how angry he really was. "We've been sleeping together. Hell, we're practically living together. In my mind, that gives you some reason to be a little jealous, to be bothered *just a little bit*. So how come you're telling me you don't care if I flirt with other women? How about if I take another woman to bed—would you have an opinion about *that?*''

"Of course I'd have an opinion about that." She drew in a shaky breath, aware that she would be putting herself at his mercy if she revealed how important he'd become to her, but unable to stop herself from admitting, "I'd *hate* it. I'd seriously consider shooting you." Her voice rose to match his. "Is that what you want to know?"

They stared at each other across the space in the room, and she couldn't stand the silence. "Can't you tell how much I've liked having you in my life? I'm truly sorry if I made you think I don't care—" She covered her face with shaking hands.

"Baby." It was a hoarse whisper as he closed the distance between them. She met him halfway, winding her arms around his back and holding him as tightly as she could.

"I'm sorry. Jack, I'm sorry...." It was an unfinished theme, cut short by his mouth descending onto hers in a frantic, ragged kiss that didn't end until she tore her mouth away, gasping for air.

"I'm sorry, too," he said. "I don't want to fight with you." He urged her backward, walking her toward the bed until she felt the mattress bumping the back of her legs. "I can't carry you tonight, but I still want you right where I've wanted you every night since we met."

He unbuttoned her blouse and slipped his hands beneath, sliding around her torso to unhook her bra, then stepping away from her long enough to take all of her clothing from her. When he started to shuck off the T-shirt he'd put on after his shower, she brushed his hands aside and removed it herself. Then she slipped her hands beneath his shorts and briefs to his buttocks, and he groaned. Gently she lowered the clothing, freeing his jutting arousal with small warm hands that lingered until he was unable to resist thrusting his hips into her palms over and over again.

Finally, he drew her hands away with a rueful smile. "If you do much more of that, this will end before we really get started."

She was kneeling before him, concentrating on easing his clothing over his injured knee. At his words, she leaned forward and placed her mouth on his heated flesh in a brief caress that made him jerk and groan again.

Taking her wrists, he drew her to her feet as he kicked away his shorts. When he slipped his big hands down her back and pressed her naked body against his, an involuntary shiver of delight ran through her. She put her hands up to his shoulders, resting her forearms against the firm muscles that covered his upper arms, and laid her head on his wide chest. Beneath her ear, his heart beat, sure and strong. She rubbed her cheek against him like a cat, loving the feel of smooth flesh beneath silky, curling hairs. Between them, the proof of his need for her pulsed insistently, and she felt him quiver when she turned her face and traced one of his small copper nipples with her tongue.

"Lie down with me." His voice was a gutteral growl that she instinctively obeyed, climbing onto the bed and waiting impatiently as he eased himself down without jostling his knee. His knee could be quite a handicap, she thought suddenly. Then again...

When he reached for her, she turned toward him, raising her leg and draping it high across his belly. Immediately he seized her by the waist and pulled her up over him so that she straddled his hips.

The sudden action startled her. After a second of battling embarrassment at the uninhibited position, she relaxed. Jack was warm and solid—very, very solid—beneath her and she realized that in this position she had far more control over the pace of their lovemaking.

He grinned, although it was more a baring of his teeth, and said, "Like it up there, do you?"

She smiled and set her palms on his nipples, rubbing in tiny circles, feeling the little nubs rising beneath her ministrations. "It's…interesting," she said. "I think I could get used to it."

"I'd be more than happy to let you practice on me anytime." He lifted his hips slightly beneath her, and she clutched at his shoulders for balance.

Leaning forward brought a whole new point of contact into play, she discovered. She looked down. At the vee of her legs, her own dark curls were a striking contrast to Jack's much lighter cloud of hair. And between them…between them, a thick column of aroused male was snugly sandwiched. Experimentally she rose onto her knees and his sex immediately sprang back to poise at the entrance to her body.

She was hot, already surprisingly wet and she couldn't wait. Slowly she lowered her body, savoring the long, sweet slide of his flesh into hers. Glancing away from the riveting sight, she surprised a fiercely exultant expression on his face, an expression which altered, lightened into That Smile. "What are you thinking?" she whispered.

He chuckled, and she caught her breath as the action rippled the heavy muscles across his belly, making him move enticingly inside her.

"I was thinking," he said in a deep, strained tone, "that we're going to have to shift into a higher speed before I burn out my gears." And with that, he took her hips firmly in his big hands, lifting her and releasing her again before restraining her with an easy grip while beneath her he began to thrust powerfully, moving in and out of her with a purposeful stroke that shattered her control. Each slam of his hips was a fresh jolt of feeling. All her body seemed to draw in, to center at the point where they met over and over again. She threw her head back, cried out, and felt within her abdomen the long, deep rhythm of contractions that shook her entire body with their strength, slowly ebbing in power until she fell forward to lie on his chest.

And only then, with the shift in position, did she realize that he was still rigid and throbbing within her.

She started to push herself into a sitting position again, but he stopped her with a gutteral "Hold still." His arms came around her like vises, one big hand splayed over her bottom pressing her more deeply around him, the other cradling her skull, holding her head against his chest.

"I don't want it to end." But his body had other ideas. Even as he spoke, she felt his hips gathering, shaking with his effort not to move, finally holding him rigid against her while the exquisite pumping of his body poured his seed into her. When he finished, his arms slowly fell away from her to lie, palms up in total relaxation, on the bed.

She lay where she was for long moments, until the harsh sounds of accelerated breathing died away and the air-conditioned room felt chilly on her backside. Slipping off him, she dragged the sheet up over them and curled against his side with her cheek on his chest and her hand on his heart.

And she slept.

Nine

Two weeks later, on a Tuesday, Jack's photographer friend, Runt, came to take the photos Jack had requested. He was manic and efficient, with a quick sense of humor, and he couldn't have looked less like his nickname, she was amused to note as he barreled around the shop, somehow managing to slip around fragile displays and glass counters while she held her breath. Built like a sumo wrestler, Runt hefted his heavy equipment as easily as…as Jack lifted her.

Just the memory of some of the times he'd lifted her made her breath come faster and her muscles loosen. She'd been long and gangly all her life. Being carried around by him like a Barbie doll was a surprisingly sensual sensation. But having Jack in her life made every day an exciting, new adventure, and she didn't mean only the wild, all-consuming hours they spent in bed…although that certainly hadn't hurt.

Jack was unpredictable, amusing, stimulating both her

mind and her body. And he enjoyed being with her, she was sure of it. She'd spent more time in a month with him than she had with Oliver in the entire eighteen months of their engagement.

Jack was also comfortable, she decided, although she wasn't sure he'd appreciate the term. With her ex-fiancé, she'd felt she always had to be scurrying around doing little housewifely chores. And taking care of his children. Which, as it turned out, was why he was going to marry her in the first place.

Still, life with Jack was comfortable. He pampered her, rubbing her feet at night when she was weary, insisting on taking a turn making meals, sneaking up behind her to slip his arms around her waist and rock her back and forth, singing some top forties hit in her ear. Last week he'd sent her a magnificent African violet with lavender blooms, and he'd taken her—along with Alexa—to an outdoor concert in a local park, where they'd watched the sun set over a lake while Pachelbel's beautiful "Canon in D" haunted the air.

Of course, she'd also sat through several lacrosse games at which she'd squeezed her eyes shut every time he took the field. His knee was nearly healed, with only some strange green and yellow bruises scattered around, and she didn't want to watch him get "creamed" again.

"Those bird thingys are great! Can we use a few of 'em?" Runt interrupted her daydreaming by pointing at a shelf of feather accessories—wouldn't you know it—on the very top shelf of her storage wall. "And tell me again what accessories will go with the dresses? I'm thinking one of those little white fake umbrellas might be nice."

Runt's powers of description needed some work, she thought as she went in search of the white parasol she kept for displays. But he seemed confident and professional, and she knew Jack trusted him. After an initial visit during which he'd decided her shop and the triple mirror in the workroom were great props, Runt had suggested that it might be easier for him to come to Frannie than the other way around.

The shoot was scheduled for 2:00 p.m. At 2:10 Jack still hadn't arrived. He wanted to supervise, to get the "look" he had in mind, he said. But he also was bringing the girl who would be modeling the gowns, so Frannie was a little concerned. It was very unlike Jack to be late. In fact, she'd learned in the three weeks they'd been together—her euphemism for their arrangement—that promptness was one of his virtues. If he said he'd be home at a certain time, he invariably was. And the one time his appointments had run late, he'd called and given her plenty of notice.

At two-fifteen, as Runt was finishing arranging his lights and the portable backdrop he'd brought, she heard Jack's van in the driveway. She hurried through the house and met him just as he was coming through the front door. The expression on his face alerted her immediately that something was wrong.

"Hi. Sorry I'm late." He dropped a distracted kiss in the general area of her lips and started through the house. "We have a problem."

"What?" She scrambled to get out of his way. A wise person didn't get in the way of Jack in a hurry. It was an invitation to get mowed down. He didn't do it on purpose, she was sure, he just didn't think about his size relative to most other people's.

"Nan has the flu."

"Oh, no! What are we going to do?" Nan was the model whom Jack had gotten to pose for the shots. He'd told her Nan owed him a favor; she wondered just how much of his business was predicated on doing people, "favors." Jack had a softer heart than he wanted to let on. She suspected a lot of the favors he performed had far more impact on the other person's life than the return favor would on Jack's.

"It's not what I'm going to do. It's what you're going to do." He stopped in the kitchen so suddenly that she nearly ran into his shoulder blades. He took her by one arm and she moved toward him, expecting a kiss, but instead he turned her in a circle, checking her over like a rancher at a horse auction.

"But I don't know any models," she protested. "Jillian's got the face and the figure for it, but she'd die before she'd crawl into a wedding gown, I think. She says she's allergic to marriage—oh, no. No, no, no," she insisted, the light dawning as Jack practically dragged her into the workroom. "I've never done this. I can't!"

"Hey, Runt."

"Hey, Jack."

"The woman I lined up got sick. We're going to use Frannie for the shoot."

"No, we are not going to use Frannie for the shoot," she insisted. "I'm not a model. I don't know how to stand. My hair's a disaster…I'm not pretty enough."

Both men stopped what they were doing and turned to look at her. She finally succeeded in freeing her wrist from Jack's grasp and she immediately backed a foot away until she banged up against the wall.

"She's kidding, right?" Runt said to Jack.

"Don't think so," Jack said. His eyes were very intent, assessing, yet filled with warmth and understanding.

"You have classic bone structure. Incredible smile. Sexy eyes. I'll just have Jack stand next to the camera when I'm shooting—I like the sparkle in your eyes when you look at him." Runt was eyeing her critically. "You just need a little makeup."

"Makeup? All right." She rose, too flustered by what he'd just said about the way she looked at Jack to continue to resist. "I'll—"

"Sit still, I'll do it. A good photographer learns makeup because you sell more stuff when the people in your shots look better than they normally do." He fished a blinding fluorescent orange nylon bag out of one of his camera cases, zipped it open and dumped onto the worktable at least twenty-five different items for making up faces. She was astonished.

And nervous, when he draped a towel around her shoulders and came at her with a cake of foundation and a sponge.

"Oh, no, I—"

"Relax. Jack, tell her to relax."

"Relax." Jack was grinning. He'd brought Alexa's baby seat into the shop so that she could watch the action, and he held the baby up toward Frannie. "Check her out, Lex. Does she look great or what?"

She glared at him. "This wouldn't be half so funny if it were happening to you."

"I know. But I'm a little too big for the gowns." He grinned again, and his genuine good humor soothed her in a strangely unexpected way. Sitting back, she let Runt do his thing.

It took him about ten minutes to brush, pat, powder and inspect. Her face felt like she had on a mask that would crack if she smiled, but when she slowly dared a change of expression, everything felt the same. When he was finished, she glanced around for a hand mirror.

Jack whistled. "You should charge for that, my friend." He looked a bit dazed, but as his eyes met hers, they gleamed with an unmistakable sexual intent. Hastily she glanced away.

Runt stood back beside Jack and nodded. "I did a pretty damn good job if I do say so myself."

Frannie sniffed. "Did I look that bad before?"

Both men looked startled. Then Jack smiled and came toward her, touching her painted lips in a bare whisper of a kiss that left her longing for more. "This is nice for special occasions, but I've always been partial to the real thing."

She was pleased all out of proportion to the simple statement, and she didn't know what to say. Luckily, Runt was issuing orders and they both turned to do his bidding.

If these photographs turned out half-decent, she'd be amazed, she thought an hour later. Runt had posed and prodded her, powdered her nose and tilted her head just so. He'd stuck a bunch of silk lilies in her hands and did God-knew-what behind her with the feathers. He'd even asked for her curling iron and did little things to her hair after he'd gotten her to tuck most of it up in what would pass for a pretty upsweep. In a photo. From a distance. She hoped.

She wished she was Alexa, whom Jack had taken upstairs for a nap halfway through this ordeal. She was exhausted. And sweaty. And incredibly uncomfortable.

The last gown they'd shot was a traditional style with a high collar and a cutout that revealed more than half her breasts before the heavier peau-de-soie satin bodice hid the goods. Had she really cut this so low on purpose? The whole thing was encrusted with seed pearls and iridescent sequins and appliqués of alençon lace. The bodice nipped in at the waist and hugged her down to her hips, where it flared into an immense, full, floor-length skirt with a cathedral train no sane bride would want to bother with. It had been a special order for a wedding that had been canceled at the last minute. She hadn't been too upset, since the bride's mother had already paid for half, and had tearfully instructed Frannie, "You can keep the dress. Burn it, resell it, I don't care. I just don't want my daughter to have to look at it and be reminded of this day." Sob, sniff, commiserate, end of conversation.

"I'll get the proofs to you sometime next week," Runt said to Jack. He was already laden down with equipment to take to his car, and Jack offered to help. She decided to stay right where she was until there was room to move again in the workroom. Jack had had to help her up onto the raised dias in front of the mirror where Runt had posed her, and she wasn't at all sure she could maneuver the dress well enough to get down without breaking her neck.

In no time at all, Runt was waving farewell and winking

at her. "Keep this guy in line. He needs a good woman to tame him."

She smiled, embarrassed that her feelings must show. "He's not the tamable type."

As Runt went out the door, she shuffled forward, feeling with her bare toes for the edge of the platform. She hadn't bothered with shoes since they wouldn't be visible, anyway. With her left hand, she grabbed handfuls of slippery peau-de-soie that she stuffed under one arm as she tried to pick up enough of the mile-long train to be able to walk. She reached for the sheer organdy veil with the other hand—and the smooth satin under her elbow all went slithering down to the floor in a vast, white puddle.

Jack walked back in from the front, where he had locked the door behind Runt. When he saw her, he started to laugh. "Need a hand?"

"Please. This is my worst nightmare. I told that woman when she insisted on this ridiculous dress that it wasn't practical. I didn't know it would be a safety hazard, though!"

Jack shoved the white cloud aside and stepped toward her, still laughing. "Come here. I'll rescue you." Setting both hands at her waist, he lifted her off her feet. She grabbed at his shoulders for balance as he pivoted and took a few steps away, setting her down next to the worktable with the train billowing out behind her.

"Thank you." And she really meant it. "If I get out of this, I swear I'll never put on another wedding gown again!" She looked up at him, laughing now, too.

"Are you sure about that?" His voice sounded funny, deep and smooth, but she didn't have a chance to speak. Lowering his head, he sought out her lips as he gathered her closely against him in a possessive grip.

"Jack, wait!" She evaded his lips, reading his intent in his eyes. "I have to get out of this dress."

"Wrong. I like you in this getup. It inspired me."

"Inspired you?" She turned her head to keep him from

capturing her in another kiss, and instead his lips fastened on her earlobe, sucking it into his mouth and swirling his tongue around the tender skin in a caress that surprised her with its erotic message.

"You made me think about what I was missing." There was a warm light in his silvery eyes as he tightened his arms around her and drew her closer again. "Marry me."

"Ma—? Have these dresses scrambled your brain?" Taking refuge in flip banter, she pushed against his chest. Her sudden action surprised him, she could see it in his eyes, and he automatically let her go. Quickly she backed away a step. She was breathless; her heart was banging so loudly she could almost hear it.

"Maybe." He closed the gap between them and placed his big hands along her cheeks, cradling her jaw. "But I mean it. Marry me, Frannie. We make a hell of a team."

Only Jack, she thought, with fleeting amusement, could relate a proposal of marriage to a sporting event. But her head was spinning and the world was whirling and as she reached up and clasped his thick wrists, he moved faster, lowering his head and taking her mouth in one of the intimate kisses that always melted her bones, her brains and any resistance she might have had. Sagging against him, she was captured by the magic that ignited, as always, when he touched her.

His hands moved from her cheeks, down her shoulders and around her back, and he pulled her as close as the petticoats beneath the dress would allow. An impatient sound rumbled up from the back of his throat. "You have on too damned many layers."

She smiled against his lips, although she was reeling in shock. "I know."

"And you haven't answered me yet."

"I know."

He kissed her again, deliberately doing his best to seduce her now. "Marry me."

When he lifted his mouth from hers, she hesitated. God,

this wasn't fair. He was offering her the moon but she knew it was an illusion. He didn't love her, though he certainly proved over and over again that he wanted her. And he needed her. She remembered Jill's warning: Don't take on this responsibility hoping it will lead to anything more. Deirdre had said he might marry again now that he had a child to care for. And he knew firsthand that she was experienced with children. Could she live with him, love him, knowing he'd married her out of practicality rather than passion? Heaven knew he hadn't had to offer her marriage to get the passion part, though she couldn't regret it. In her heart, she'd said, "I do," the night he'd first made her his, committing herself to him and only him.

So, the question wasn't whether or not she wanted to marry him. Rather, she had to ask herself if she could take him for her husband for the rest of her life, knowing she could never say the simple words of love any other woman took as her right? Never hear them?

The possibility of heartbreak seemed more like a promise. But down the other road to her future lay a lonely path empty of children, of warm companionship, of the intense sexual fulfillment no one but Jack would ever be able to give her.

And she loved him.

She took a deep breath and met his silver gaze, tossing good sense and caution to the floor to join the yards of fabric in which they stood. "All right. I'll marry you."

He went completely still when she uttered the words. For a long moment he was a man of marble, still and frozen. Then his chest rose and fell in one deep breath. He threw back his head, right there in her workroom, and howled. Loudly. Wolf-wailing-at-the-moon loudly.

"Sh-h-h! You'll wake the baby!" She was just starting to giggle when he covered her mouth with his own again, lifting her off her feet and bending her backward over his arm so that she clutched at his neck to regain her balance. His mouth was a hot, hungry animal devouring her response, drinking in the little noises she couldn't hold back, invading the fortress behind her teeth with such devastating surety that she never thought of putting up a defense.

He turned and set her on the edge of the workbench, though he kept her so deeply immersed in kisses that she barely recognized the motion. His arms loosened slowly, stroking over the slippery satin and running up and down her back, then moving around her torso to her ribs, finally arriving at his ultimate destination as he dipped below the daring cutout neck of the dress to palm her breasts, lifting them out of their confinement and into his hands. His thumbs brushed back and forth, calling her nipples to his touch, and she nearly leaped off the bench as the stimulation spread a rioting radius of sensation rolling outward, unerringly arrowing down to concentrate at the waiting portal of her body. Then his mouth left hers and fastened fiercely on one peaked crest, suckling so strongly she almost screamed aloud. As it was, she moaned wildly, spreading her fingers and spearing them through his hair, keeping his head a prisoner at her breast.

He surged against her, spreading her thighs with the pressure of his body, moving between her legs only to be foiled by the fabric between them. She shifted and took her hands from his head, gripping the edge of the table and pushing herself against him, and without warning, he was a blur of movement, a whirlwind of action, pulling the white skirts up and shoving them behind her, inexorably removing barrier after barrier until she felt the rough fabric of his slacks grazing against the tender flesh of her inner thighs. He surged against her once and then slipped fluidly out of her grasp, down her body, pressing hot kisses against her through the satin until his mouth was suddenly, shockingly nuzzling at the aching feminine flesh between her legs, his breath burning her through her thin panties and his tongue licking insistently against the fabric, dampening it in his quest for her essence. His palms settled against her inner thighs, holding her open to his skillful ministrations as he nibbled and licked until he located the throbbing nub of her desire, settling around her and playing her with devastating precision.

Then she did cry out, throwing her head back and bracing herself on her hands, pushing her body forward, mutely begging for him to assuage her longing. With a deep, incoherent sound, he rose, tearing at his pants, then the flimsy fabric of her panties, rending them and tossing them aside in one smooth motion that demonstrated vividly the power he held in check.

She had a second's view of his blazing eyes as he leaned over her, his hand between them guiding himself to the entrance of her body without hesitation, then without a second's delay, he shoved forward, grasping her hips and pulling her onto him. She let the force of his big body carry her backward until she was lying on the table, anchored to earth only by the ferocious pounding of his hard, sizzling flesh that crowded into her until she was nothing but his, a receptacle for his taking, begging him with incoherent sounds of surrender to give her what she needed. He hung over her, his gaze drinking in her response, his body surrounded by her, and she knew a deep, feminine satisfaction within her as she read his eyes correctly, wrapping her bared legs around his back and tilting herself upward, wordlessly encouraging him to give in to the shaking, speeding rhythm of his hips. He shoved his hands beneath her, grasping her buttocks and pulling them wide and the unaccustomed sensation opened her mouth in a soundless scream as her own body began its inevitable rush toward climax, meeting and squeezing his jerking, thrusting flesh as he arched his back in age-old masculine ecstasy and poured his seed into the waiting vessel of her womb.

She lay on the worktable afterward, with Jack slumped over her body, his gasping, panting breaths both reasssuring and pleasing. Her body pulsed one final time and he grunted, jerking against her as his supersensitized flesh registered the sensation. She scratched her nails over his back in the private after-loving ritual they'd established, making random little circles at a leisurely pace, and he sighed, turning his head to kiss the breast that lay beneath his cheek.

Then he pulled himself up on his elbows over her, with a self-satisfied grin flashing over his face as he said, "You'll never stand at this table again without thinking of me."

She smiled faintly as the red haze of need receded and the world came back into focus. "I may never stand at this table again, period."

To her incredulous surprise, his face grew red and he ducked his head. "Sorry. I got a little carried away, I guess." Then he looked up, and that unreadable intense look was back in his eyes as he said, "You're the only woman in the world who can do that to me."

Again she didn't know how to respond, but he didn't give her a chance, lifting himself away from her and propping her in a sitting position while he closed his pants. She leaned her head on his chest, exhaustion creeping into all her muscles as he looked down at the back of her neck and carefully opened the fastenings that held her inside the satin casing.

"Will you wear this one?"

"What?" She was drained, dull, her brain sluggishly wrapping itself around the request.

"When we get married, will you wear this one?"

Startled into wakefulness, she shook her head. "This is the most impractical gown—"

"But think of the memories." He looked into her face with earnest eyes and she remembered suddenly why she needed to be alert around him. With little effort, he probably could charm her into agreeing to swim naked in the Choptank River at high noon in front of a boatload of fishermen. "You and I will say our vows thinking of how you agreed to marry me in this dress. I'll be thinking about the way your sweet little—"

"Do you realize it will take five people to carry this train?"

"I'll call a couple of the guys on the team."

"All right! You win—I'll wear the dress. Just don't blame me when this train wraps around your ankles and trips you up," she said darkly. Then reality slapped her in the face and she realized what they were talking about.

A wedding. A marriage.

"Jack…" She couldn't disguise the troubled note in her voice. "Maybe we should think about this."

"I don't need to think. This wasn't a snap decision." His words pierced the air above her head. Beneath her ear, his heart still pumped madly in his chest. "I want to marry you, Frannie. We like each other. We both care about making a good life for Lex. I'd like to have more children, and I think you would, too. We're great together in bed." He looked around them and a whimsical smile crossed his face. "And out."

"I know, but maybe those aren't good rea—"

"They're important reasons. They'll last for a lifetime."

She looked up into his face, drinking in the sight of his blunt, beloved features, knowing that not one of those was the reason she was saying yes. "If you're sure you've thought about what you're taking on…I want to marry you." She took one of his hands in hers and raised it to her lips, kissing the tough pad of flesh at the base of his palm. If she kept things light, pleasant, organized, maybe this would work out. "I wonder what you'll look like with gray hair."

His eyes warmed, danced. "About the same as you, baby cakes." He stepped back and lifted her to the floor. "I'll check with the justice of the peace, see what's required for a license, and how long we have to wait."

"Jack…" She raised her head from unfastening the tight buttons at the wrists of the dress. "I'm not going to back out. We don't have to plan the entire wedding this minute."

"Yes, we do." He tipped her chin up with his index

finger and kissed her, a lingering, hungry kiss that left her clinging to him again in limp surrender. "We didn't use anything tonight, and I'm damn sure you weren't any more prepared than I was last week. If we've made a little brother or sister for Lex, it's going to be legitimate. Besides—" and he flashed the confident, cocky grin that she so loved "—we already know we're great parents. Why wait to join forces?"

She knew there was a possibility she could have conceived. She knew she shouldn't hope so, it would be insane with Alexa barely a year old when their baby would be born, but oh, God! Please. She'd wanted a baby of her own all her life, wanted to be pregnant, to feel a new person growing inside her. Having Jack's baby would be the culmination of the best thing that had ever happened to her. Ever.

"You're right," she said. "So you don't want a church wedding?"

He shrugged. "Not unless you do. I just want to get married as fast as possible."

She'd always assumed that when she married—if she married—she would walk down the short, wide aisle in the little country church near her family's home wearing white. Something she'd made for herself. Something special. Jack didn't sound as though he had even considered a church wedding. And he wanted her to wear a dress she'd designed for another woman, a dress she would never have chosen unless she'd lost her mind.

But he liked the dress. At least it was white. And he was right. It would hold special memories for them.

And when she thought about planning a wedding, pretending to her family and friends that they were getting married for the normal reasons any other couple did, she realized that she would rather do this quickly and quietly. She'd have enough questions to answer later.

"I don't care, either," she said.

* * *

Good news—or good gossip—spread like wildfire, and it wasn't a day before people were congratulating him. It was a good feeling. Especially considering how strange Frannie had been acting.

When he'd suggested she call her family, she'd calmly told him there was no rush, that they could wait until they were married to share the news. He'd disagreed; having had one experience with shocking Donald was enough. He insisted until she finally gave in and called them, first Billy, then Donald and Robert, and after she'd told them her news, he'd asked to speak to them. Billy couldn't have been more tickled. Donald and Robert were slightly more reserved, though Donald thawed a bit when Jack assured him he would take good care of his sister. Robert, whom he had never met, didn't beat around the bush.

"Donald tells me Frannie will be stepping right into motherhood," he said.

"In a manner of speaking." Jack hoped Frannie couldn't hear the conversation. Lex had started to holler and she'd walked over to take her out of her infant seat.

"I hope you're not doing this for free baby-sitting."

"No more than you were all the years she helped you out." Robert had to be the most selfish jerk alive. Didn't he realize how offensive his words were to his sister? "And I didn't have to marry her to get baby-sitting or anything else," he said. "I don't know you, but I expect that when we meet, you'll be happy for your sister." He deliberately allowed his tone to express aggression, practically growling out the last word.

After a second of silence, Robert's voice came back over the line, sounding far more subdued than he had when the conversation started. "Of course I'm happy for Frannie. I just felt that I had to be sure you were—"

"Thank you," Jack said, smoothly cutting him off. "I'm looking forward to meeting you, too." And if there was a veiled threat in his tone, he figured Robert deserved to sweat a little bit. Selfish brat.

He put down the phone and turned to Frannie, who was bouncing Lex on her hip and singing to her. "Mission accomplished."

She smiled, apparently unaware of the conversation that had just passed between her brother and him. "I'm glad we called them. Now I don't feel like I'm sneaking around behind their backs. Donald wanted to know when the wedding would be. I told him we'd let him know."

"And we will." He grinned. "Afterward."

Once he got her going, she insisted they tell her two closest friends, Deirdre and Jillian. That led to a dinner invitation for both women the following evening.

Dinner with Frannie's best friends. He took a deep breath, well aware that this could be even worse than dealing with her brothers. A lot worse.

He liked Deirdre. They'd been neighbors and friends as kids, and she'd always been one of the sweetest women he knew. He wasn't certain yet how he felt about Jillian. He knew her in passing; they'd done some business together and he'd found her pleasant, with a good sense of humor. But she had a reputation for chewing men up and spitting them out mangled, and he'd always steered clear. Besides, blond ice maidens weren't his type. He preferred long, leggy brunettes with pouty lips and chocolate eyes.

The evening they came to dinner, he volunteered to barbecue chicken on the grill, figuring that would give the three women some uninterrupted talk time. To his surprise, Frannie had things completely prepared before either of them arrived, and she ushered them right out to the patio behind her house, where he was just starting the chicken.

With her usual timing, Alexa's waking coos could be heard over the baby monitor from the bedroom where she'd been napping.

"Uh-oh, someone's awake," Frannie said. "No, Jack, you entertain. I'll be back in a minute." And she vanished.

"Dee." He moved toward the shortest woman, pulling her into a hug when she held out her hand. He felt her stiffen for a moment, and he mentally cursed the husband who'd dumped her. What else had the guy done to her to make her afraid of a hug?

When he tugged affectionately on her long black braid, she finally relaxed and hugged him back. "Hi, Jack, it's good to see you."

"It's good to see you, too," he told her, assessing the shadows beneath her green eyes. "Where are Heckyl and Jeckyl?"

She laughed at the reference to her preschool-age sons. "The boys went to my mother's tonight. I hate to inflict them on her, but she was at the house when Frannie called and she insisted on taking them tonight, so I could 'visit.' Bless her heart." Then she sobered. "Jack, I can't thank you enough for getting me into the farmhouse. It's perfect, and the boys love it out in the country."

"Translation," said Jillian from behind her. "There's plenty to do, which keeps them out of trouble." She walked around the table and held out her hand. "Hello, Jack."

"Jillian." He took the hand rather than hugging her as he had Dee. He got the feeling no one hugged this woman without receiving permission first.

"So," she said briskly, "why do you want to marry Frannie?"

"Jill!" Dee shook her finger at her friend. "You promised not to cross-examine him."

"This isn't a cross-exam," the blonde said in a reasonable tone. "Is it, Jack?"

He laughed. "Not yet."

"So...?" She wasn't going to let it slide.

He took a deep breath, hoping she wasn't going to try to pin him down. "Isn't it obvious? Frannie's warm and giving, everything I could ever want in a wife. It's not every woman who would take a man with a three-month-old."

To his surprise, Jillian's eyes softened. "You might be surprised."

Lannette leaped into his mind. "I doubt it."

"And look who's here." They all turned as Frannie came outside, carrying the baby. "It's your auntie Dee and auntie Jill."

"And we are going to spoil you rotten, kiddo." Jillian practically leaped around the table. "Give," she said to Frannie.

He was surprised even further. He never would have pegged Jillian Kerr for the motherly type. Her friendship with Frannie suddenly made more sense to him. Before, he couldn't quite imagine someone like her being a good friend to Frannie.

The evening passed pleasantly, with both women offering congratulations before the conversation turned to general topics. Frannie made no effort to speak to either of her friends alone; in fact, she almost—to him, anyway—appeared to want to avoid opportunities for personal moments.

When the evening ended and the door closed, he took her in his arms, rocking her back and forth against his chest. "Have we told all the important people in your life? I'm not sure I can take being examined for flaws many more times."

Her arms were linked around his neck, and her head tilted back so she could see his face. "What? Jack Ferris worrying about flaws? I thought you were perfect."

"Not likely." He speared his fingers through her hair to cradle her skull. "If I was, I'd have married you the first time around."

"You didn't know me then," she pointed out.

"No, but if I were perfect, I'd have found you." He put his hands beneath her bottom and lifted her and she automatically clasped her legs around his waist. He was already carrying her toward the stairs as he said, "Wanta go to bed?"

Later, as he lay spent and sweating, cuddling her pretty body, he decided he was the luckiest man in the world to have found Frannie. "You're the best thing that ever happened to me," he told her.

And even in the darkness, he could hear the happiness in her voice as she said, "I'm glad."

Ten

He got a license for a Tuesday only a week away. Frannie sent the infamous wedding dress to the cleaner and worried about how she would find time to modify the train enough to make it manageable. They asked Stu, Dee and Jillian to be witnesses and made arrangements for a small lunch afterward.

They talked about how to consolidate their households and decided it made more sense to move into Frannie's larger house, particularly since her business was there, as well. Half his things had migrated there already, anyhow. She informed him that it made no sense to pursue a day care for Alexa, that it would be cheaper simply to hire someone to help care for the baby in their home, literally only a few steps away from her shop. He informed her that if she wasn't pregnant already, he wanted to wait a little while, give them a chance to enjoy each other before adding another child to the household.

They started packing up his condo, making decisions on what to keep and what to part with.

"Your dishes match," he said to her on the Thursday evening before the wedding. "Can't we just throw mine away?"

"Good try," she said, wrapping newspaper around a coffee cup. "We're donating these to the senior center, remember? They don't care if dishes don't match."

"Neither did I," he said. He rose to his feet as she placed the cup in a box loaded with dishware. "Let me put these in the van. Then you can drive down to the center and get someone to carry them in for you, while Stu and I unhook the CD speakers, the stereo and the VCR and stick them in the other van."

She nodded. "I'll leave the baby here since she seems happy." With a wave she went out the front door, leaving it propped open as it had been all evening. He gazed after her for a moment, fighting the urge to follow and drag her to him for a kiss. She never kissed him before she left him unless he initiated it. In fact, she rarely ever kissed him unless he started it. And it wasn't that she disliked it. Whenever he reached for her, she came into his arms eagerly, returning his caresses.

So what was holding her back? He sensed that she would like to be more affectionate, that she was holding herself in check. He'd shown her every way he knew how that she was the most important thing in his life, that he needed her and wanted her. Was she holding out on him because he hadn't declared his undying love?

Love. His lip curled. Just because he hadn't said some dumb little words didn't mean he wasn't committed to her for the rest of his life. What he and Frannie had was better than love, and a hell of a lot less fragile. They hardly ever fought. If they were in love, they'd probably fight all the time. No sir, they didn't need love. They were doing great together without anybody's hearts getting in the way.

"I think I've got it." Stu's voice floated up from the

basement. "Pull on the cable by the TV and see what happens."

It was the right one, and Stu came up to help him carefully box up his precious electronic equipment. Frannie had a disgraceful excuse for a stereo that was going in the trash, regardless of whom she thought she might donate it to. He wouldn't give that thing to anybody on purpose.

"The big day is looming on the horizon," Stu commented. "Are you getting scared?"

"Nope." Jack set the VCR in the box and started stuffing newspaper around it. "I am ready to tie the knot, my friend. Ready for marital bliss."

Stu sat back on his heels. "I never thought I'd hear those words from you. I figured you'd never let yourself fall in love again."

"Fall in love? Love doesn't have a thing to do with this marriage," he said. "You know how it is. If I have to get married again, I'm going to do it the smart way. This time I made sure we're compatible before the question of marriage came up."

"You're kidding me, right?" Stu shot him a troubled glance. "If it's that big a deal, why bother? You don't have to get married again."

"I do." He taped the box shut and ripped the tape away with unnecessary force. "I don't want Lex to grow up without a mother. And brothers and sisters. And besides, Frannie and I are friends. We get along better than we ever would if we were in love."

"Are you telling me any woman would do?"

"No, but I'm sure there were a number of them around who would have fit the bill."

Liar. He recognized the untruth before it even reached Stu's ears. But *admitting,* even to himself, that Frannie was the only woman he would ever want again, was too scary to face. Too risky. He didn't need risk; he had everything he could want.

But Stu looked appalled. "Does Frannie know you assessed her and she came out with a good rating? What'd you do, on a scale of one to ten, how beautiful—''

"A beautiful woman isn't a perfect one." His voice was mild. Since he'd met Frannie, Lannette's power over him seemed to have dwindled to a very occasional, regretful twinge. The bitterness and anger that he'd nursed inside for so long simply seemed like too much effort. "And no, it doesn't particularly matter what she looks like. We're the best of friends, we enjoy being together, and to top it off, there's the chemistry...."

"The chemistry." Stu's voice went syrupy and soft. "Everybody knows the chemistry between you two is great, bud. You practically foam at the mouth when you spot her, and she looks at you like you're the only man on the planet." Stu paused and shook his head. "If I didn't know you'd sworn off it, I'd swear you were in love with her."

The statement made Jack uneasy. "We're not getting married for love. I did that once before and found out my judgment was lousy. This time I'm marrying for the right reasons."

Stu was staring at him, frowning. "Which are...."

"Companionship, sex and great parenting skills."

He never knew what made him look up at that exact instant. Frannie stood in the doorway, one hand over her mouth, the fingers gripping her cheeks so tightly he could see the indentations in her fine skin. Above the hand, her face was white, a dull, shocked abnormal white around eyes gone so dark and dead that it frightened him.

"Baby—" He half rose, extending a hand. Beside him, Stu uttered a shocked exclamation, but Jack was oblivious to it. All that mattered to him was making her understand what she'd overheard, what she'd obviously misunderstood. Misunderstood? screamed his conscience. He took a step toward her.

And she bolted. In the time it took him to process the sounds he heard, she cleared the front door and threw herself into her van. He recovered enough to start to go after her, but as he reached the door, she fumbled her keys into the ignition and started the van with a roar, then backed out of his driveway wildly and took off.

What had he done?

His hands shook as he scrubbed them over his face. He turned back to Stu. "She heard...oh, God, she heard."

"So?"

He whipped up his head to stare hard at his buddy. "What did you say?"

"I said 'So' as in 'So what?'" Stu's face was set and angry, a look in his eyes Jack had never seen before off the lacrosse field. "You don't love her. She might as well know the score going in. You're right. You wouldn't want to love Frannie like you loved Lannette. *But you should love her for herself.* Because she's twice the woman your twitty ex was." Stu set down the speaker he was still holding. "Since it looks like you won't be moving after all, I'm going home. To the wife who loves me enough to put up with a weird-colored house because I love her, too."

He stomped out the still-open door as Jack sat numbly on the floor, the truth hitting him in great pounding hammers of reality.

Frannie wasn't Lannette.

The truth was a brutal revelation.

He'd been brutal. He'd killed the softer part of himself that once had believed in love and told himself she was a great companion. She understood him, she cared about his problems, she adored his niece. And the fact that they were so hot together in bed they damn near set the sheets afire, he'd figured was simple chemistry and incredible good fortune.

Well, that was true. She was all those things. Because she loved him.

She had plenty of friends. She didn't need another friend. She needed someone who loved her...she needed *him*.

And he needed her. She'd brought warmth and depth back into his life; he'd been simply skating over the surface. She completed him in a way no other woman ever had, ever could.

Where would she go? He had to get her to come back, to listen, to forgive. His hands were still shaking as he reached for the telephone and the city directory.

She had nowhere to go, she thought, her mind madly ticking over the possibilities. She couldn't go home, that was the first place Jack would look.

And her family was out, as were Dee and Jill, even April. She wouldn't underestimate his power to charm her whereabouts out of any of them. Of course, that was assuming he even cared enough to look. Jack had more than his share of pride, and she doubted he'd be willing to broadcast the fact that he didn't have a clue about where his fiancée had gotten to.

No, she wouldn't underestimate that formidable charm ever again. Nor the formidable mind behind it. She swung onto the beltway on-ramp, driving aimlessly, her chest heaving as she fought for self-control.

Oh, he'd outmaneuvered her at every junction in their relationship, manipulated her every decision, every thought. And he'd done it on purpose.

Funny how it was so easy to see when she looked back. She'd willingly fallen into the role of baby-sitter. He hadn't given her time to think. No, he'd used the intensity of the attraction she felt to propel her into his arms, and then he'd moved so fast she didn't even see it coming, wrapping her in false intimacy that she had believed was real. He'd all but moved into her house well before he'd proposed, he'd treated her like his missing half until she began to believe it. She'd even begun to hope that someday he might be able to return her love, so convincing had he been. He'd lulled her into believing he really wanted *her*, just like Oliver had.

Her eyes burned but she'd die before she'd cry over him. The time on the dashboard clock caught her eye. Alexa should be getting hungry soon— She caught herself. Alexa wasn't hers. She had no one to worry over, no one to cuddle, to make bottles or meals for...she had no one.

Her breath caught on a dry sob and her stomach heaved. Fiercely she swallowed, refusing either to cry or throw up. She needed to find a place to think, to decide what to do. Instinct told her to flee. Keep going and never look back. Leave the city, the state, the country.

If only it were that easy. What would it be like to simply quit your life and start fresh somewhere else? Somewhere where no one knew you, knew that twice you'd been engaged to men who didn't love you, men who only wanted a baby-sitter with the added convenience of regular sex.

She wasn't a quitter, had never been one to give up in her entire life. Not when her mother died, not when her father died. Even when Oliver broke their engagement to marry someone he'd fallen in love with, she hadn't given up, but had simply changed her dream, gone back to school and started doing what she'd always loved.

She had no dreams to pursue anymore.

An exit sign loomed, drawing her attention back to the road. She was near Timonium, and she started scanning the buildings along the beltway for a motel or hotel, a place where she could be invisible, just for one night. She could afford it. And thankfully, the business load was light right now. April would be okay if she called her and told her she wouldn't be in tomorrow, that she'd see her on Monday.

All she needed was a little time to peel away any vestiges of the dream she'd shared with Jack.

Deirdre's phone rang about 9:00 p.m. As she leaped to answer it, Jack gripped the edges of his chair so hard his fingertips hurt. Across from him, Jillian divided her time between giving him evil glares and rocking Alexa, asleep in her arms.

"Oh, honey," Dee said. "I know. So does Jill. Are you all right? Where are you?"

He was on his feet before he realized it, striding across the room. Deirdre put out one small hand like a traffic cop denying him the right to pass. She shook her head fiercely and hunched one shoulder away from him so he couldn't take the phone from her.

She spoke again. "Jack told us. He's terribly worried—"

She broke off and listened again, then said, "Do you want to come here? Or to Jill's? Jack's here but he'll leave if we ask him to...yes, it does matter...all right, but call me in the morning so we know you're okay. Otherwise, I'm calling the police and reporting you missing...okay. Goodbye."

He had never felt so powerless before, not even when Lannette had walked out. Then he'd been furious and hurt—and humiliated, mostly. He hadn't been afraid that his whole life was coming to an end.

He'd lived through ten hells in the past three hours, worrying that Frannie had had an accident, that she was dead or lying alone somewhere on a road or in a hospital where no one knew her.

"Where is she?" he demanded hoarsely. "Is she all right?" He grabbed his keys from the table, ready to head out the door the second he found out where she was.

"She sounds okay." Deirdre put the phone back in its cradle and dragged quirking curls of black hair away from her eyes. She dropped onto a chair with a huge sigh and laid her head in her folded arms. "She's in a motel. She wouldn't say where. She's going to call again in the morning."

Disappointment was such a bitter taste in his throat that he turned away from the two women, looking out Deirdre's kitchen window to the fields beyond her yard. "Did she say anything else?"

Silence. Then Dee's soft voice: "She said she'll be back by Monday, that April will take care of the shop tomorrow.

She wants you to move your things out right away. Leave the key on the hall table. She says you don't need to worry, that she'll be fine.'' She stopped and he realized Deirdre was crying, her voice thickening with the sobs she couldn't hold back. "But she won't be. If you don't fix this, Jack, she'll never be fine again.''

God, could he feel any worse?

Jillian made an involuntary sound and rose from the rocking chair to put her arm over Dee's shaking shoulders. Over her head, her eyes bored into him like laser drills into steel. "You're not going to move out, are you?"

He shook his head. "Not until I've talked to her. After she listens, if she never wants to see me again, I'll honor her wishes." But he hoped to God it wouldn't come to that. He felt like his future was a shining coin flipping through the air. Heads, he won, tails, he lost.

"Good." Her voice was sober. "If I thought for a second you didn't love her, I'd kill you, Jack. I really would. But any idiot could see that you two loved each other. How could you be such an ass?"

He shook his head. "I wish I knew." But he did know. He'd been so damned busy insulating himself against the possibility of hurt that he'd destroyed the woman he was too stupid to admit he loved.

"...with kids."

He looked up. Jillian was speaking and he chopped a hand through the air impatiently. "I didn't hear you. Start over."

"I said, 'It's bad enough that she had one man who only wanted her for her way with kids.'" Her eyes were a stormy blue, telegraphing helpless fury. "Now it's happened twice."

"What other man?" His antennae went up.

Dee raised her head to stare at him. "You don't know about—"

"If I knew, why would I have asked?" he roared, patience exhausted. Dee jumped, but Jillian's eyes gleamed as if she relished a good fight.

"Frannie was engaged a few years ago. The guy was the first man she had ever been seriously interested in, because she was always too wrapped up in taking care of her family to date much. He was a widower with two little girls."

"He ditched her when he met some other woman," Dee said baldly. "He told Frannie he was sorry but that he didn't love her, that he'd admired her capacity for creating a home and caring for a family. The jerk actually told her he'd like her to meet the woman he loved, that he was sure they'd get to be good friends."

"That's when she left Taneytown," Jill added. "She went back to school full-time for two years and then started this business. She was just starting to feel good about herself again when you came along."

Jack felt sick inside. Why hadn't she told him? He'd pressed and pressed until she'd let down her defenses and let herself trust him, and then he'd treated her like she was disposable. And replaceable. If only he'd known—what? What would he have done differently?

The question couldn't be answered. But he knew that if she couldn't forgive him, his life wouldn't be worth living. Even with Alexa's presence, he'd just be going through the motions year after lonely year.

It was the longest weekend of her life. She stayed away for three nights. She bought books to read, watched movies and took walks. She went to the mall in Columbia and wandered around but when she realized she kept floating into the baby department in the big stores, she left. She should have been in Bridals, checking out the new styles and getting ideas, but she couldn't face wedding dresses right now.

Wedding gowns inevitably reminded her of the one she'd worn that Jack had enjoyed so much. And each time she let that memory float to the surface, she wanted to cry again. That stupid gown must be cursed, ruining every wedding for which it was intended.

But she didn't cry. Though the lump in her chest had grown so hard and heavy it would probably need to be removed surgically, she took a certain grim comfort from knowing that he hadn't made her cry.

She checked out of the hotel on Sunday, but she didn't go home until evening for fear that she might have to see Jack moving his things out. Around six that evening, she finally pulled her van into the driveway beside the entrance to her home. The house was dark and closed.

Inside, she flipped on the entry light and walked to the phone. On the table lay a key—Jack's key—and the lump swelled again, invading her throat. Using a pad of paper, she pushed it off the edge of the table into a drawer, which she closed. It might be stupid, but she couldn't bring herself to touch it, to pick it up knowing that Jack's hands had touched it last. She put both hands on the table and took deep breaths, forcing herself to think of nothing, of anything other than that key—until she could breathe without her breath catching.

"Are you all right?"

She jumped and whirled around. The deep, quiet voice was a shock, both because she recognized it and because she'd thought she was alone. Her heart started to race, and she swallowed as her stomach rolled. "Why are you here?"

"I'd like to talk to you," Jack said.

After one brief glance she couldn't look at him, and her gaze skittered madly over one thing, then another. "Where's Alexa?"

"Jillian's baby-sitting."

Jillian? There were too many questions attached to that answer, so she ignored them. "Where's your van?"

"I got a ride over. I was afraid if you saw it, you wouldn't come in."

She had herself under control now, and she was determined to stay that way. It was important to her that he not know how deeply he'd hurt her. "Why wouldn't I come in?" she asked, striving for a pleasant, reasonable tone. "I live here, remember?"

He ignored the rhetorical questions and took a step toward her.

She stepped back instinctively, knowing that if he touched her, her precarious hold on her self-control would fly away. "Jack, I really don't have anything to say to you. I wish you well and—"

"You don't have to say anything. I'm asking you to listen. Frannie, please."

His voice was low and quiet, so sincere that she had to grit her teeth against the sudden urge to smack his face. How dare he come here? How dare he use that intimate, "trust me" tone with her?

"No," she said. "I have a lot to do before the shop opens tomorrow." She turned her back to him and put her hand on the doorknob, wishing she were big enough to throw him out. But that would require energy, which she simply couldn't muster right now.

"You aren't going to open the shop tomorrow, remember? You're closed until Wednesday." His tone was still low and soothing, and she realized he'd moved to stand directly behind her.

"Jack," she said, and the weariness in her soul colored her voice, "I'm not going to marry you. If you have a shred of decency in you, you'll let me alone right now. I don't want to dissect what happened. I don't need an explanation. I just want to get on with my life. Please. Go."

"My first wife walked out on me, did you know that?"

She didn't answer; she couldn't tell him she knew because she was too busy fighting the waves of misery that lapped at the edges of her self-control.

"For a long time, I said I'd never get married again. And when I finally got myself together, I decided I wasn't ever going to care about a woman that way again." He paused. "And I've never felt that way about anyone else."

Her hands flew from the doorknob to cover her mouth as she absorbed the cruel words.

Jack paused as he saw her shoulders shake, but he couldn't afford to stop. If she didn't listen now, he doubted he'd ever get another chance. "I've never felt that way, because that was a silly infatuation that never should have gone any farther than a few dates. What I feel for you is so much stronger, and deeper, than I've ever known before, that it scared the hell out of me. I ran and hid rather than face being vulnerable again."

She was still now, as motionless as a statue, but at least she was listening. "I need you, baby. And you need me. I can't live without you. It's that simple." He lifted his hands, hesitated and placed them on her shoulders, ignoring her flinch. "That's why I asked you to marry me." Gently he put a little pressure into his grip, turning her around, and she let him.

He knew the beginnings of relief. She was listening; she was going to let him explain, and then everything would be right again.

Then he caught sight of her face, and a deep, crippling fear paralyzed him.

Her dark eyes harbored a deeper hurt than he'd ever imagined. Her lip trembled. "You *didn't* ask me to marry you. You issued a command. I said yes because I loved you. Even knowing that all I was to you was a built-in baby-sitter/bed partner, I said yes." A sob escaped her and she stuffed a fist against her mouth. For a long moment they stared at each other, regret and grief and rage thickening the air to a tense soup of emotion. And then she began to cry, soundlessly weeping as tears formed huge shiny puddles in her eyes and began to roll down her cheeks. She whirled again to stand with her back to him, and sobs began to punctuate her silent anguish.

He was devastated. For the first time he began to understand what he'd done to her. How deeply he'd hurt her. He'd seen her cry only once before, and it had torn him apart. And *that* night—after the first time he'd met her family—she'd been upset with herself, not him. Lannette had cried frequently, copiously, and the length of time the tears had lasted was usually the same length of time it took her to steer him into doing whatever she wanted.

Frannie's tears weren't directed at him. In fact, she tried desperately not to let him see that she was crying.

"Frannie…baby…" He took her by the shoulders and turned her around, gathering her against his chest, feeling her rigid body refusing his comfort. His own voice shook as he whispered, "I'm sorry. Please don't leave me. I need you."

She shook her head violently and pulled away from him, no longer trying to hide or stem her tears. "No, Jack. You don't *need* me. You *want* me. There's a big difference. It's called, 'love.'" Despair drew her face into a mask of terrible sadness. "I *needed* you. I thought I loved you so much that it didn't matter. But it does matter, Jack. I can't live with the man I love, knowing I'm nothing more than the one who 'fit the bill.'" She paused, then turned away again, clearly ending the confrontation. "All I ever wanted was love."

Panic gripped him, a bottomless pit of fright. "How could I be such a fool?" he said aloud. "I'm losing you, aren't I? I do love you, Frannie. I—"

"Don't you *dare* tell me that now!" She flew at him so suddenly he barely got his hands up in time to prevent her from slugging him. "Don't you dare pull a cheap stunt like that!"

She was flailing wildly at him. In self-defense, he caught her fists within his much larger ones, pulling them behind her back and anchoring them both with one hand. Her body was flush against his, and immediately his own flesh began to respond the way it always did to her. When she abruptly stopped writhing against him, he knew she'd noticed.

"If I were pulling a cheap stunt," he said, "I'd have told you a long time ago that I loved you, wouldn't I? To cement the relationship, I mean—make sure you were really on the hook. Why would I wait until Stu hit me over the head to get me to admit it? And if any woman would do, why did I eat humble pie for your damned, unforgiving, overprotective friends just to try to get you back?''

He realized he was shouting and he deliberately took a deep breath and lowered his voice. ''This is what you do to me.'' He thrust his hips gently against her, seeing the clouds of arousal in her eyes even through the tears. ''No other woman. Just you. Because this means nothing unless it's done with love.''

His grip loosened and he released her hands, stepping back and freeing her. He wanted to overwhelm her with his love, take her right here in the hallway and show her with his body how much she meant to him. But she had to want it, too. She had to believe him.

''I love you,'' he said, standing quietly with his hands at his sides. ''And I want to marry you, not because I need a baby-sitter—or a sexual playmate—but because half of me was missing when you were. I need you to make me whole again.''

She'd been staring at him during his speech; now she looked down, veiling the beautiful brown eyes that might gave him a clue about what she was thinking. When she raised her gaze to his again, his heart sank at the pain still haunting her eyes.

''I thought you might be able to love me,'' she said, ''someday. I was prepared to wait, hoping that someday you could return it.'' Her face began to lose its pinched, unhappy look and the devastation in her eyes lightened. ''It's a little overwhelming to find that someday has arrived.''

''I know exactly when I realized that I felt something more for you than I ever had for anyone,'' he said. He sensed she was weakening in her denial of him; he just hoped it was enough. ''When we took Alexa to the hospital, and the doctor assumed we were married, I wished it were true. I looked at you and decided that you were going to be mine." He paused, eyeing the space between them, then took a step toward her and held out his arms. "Would you please come over here and tell me you forgive me?"

She came into his arms, her breath shuddering out in a painful-sounding sigh as she wound her arms around his neck. Her grasp was so tight it was almost uncomfortable, but he didn't care. He pulled her against him equally tightly.

"I thought I would never do this again," she said.

"I was terrified I would never get to do this again." Slowly he closed the gap between their lips, settling his mouth on hers in a simple, tender caress meant to reassure. But when she melted against him, murmuring deep in her throat and opening her mouth for his tongue, he took everything she offered, holding her against him so that she couldn't miss the way his body wanted this day to end.

He lifted his head a fraction. "I love you," he said. "Do you still love me?"

"I have to," she said simply. "Without you, life would mean nothing."

The answer pleased him; his whole body relaxed. He hadn't realized how tense he was, waiting for her answer. "You're still marrying me on Tuesday."

Her lips curved beneath his. "There you go again, giving me orders. Don't you know how to phrase a question?"

He bent and scooped her into his arms, holding her against his heart as he walked toward the stairs, whispering into her ear.

Her laughter rang out, filling the house with love. "That wasn't the question I had in mind!"

Epilogue

She got her church wedding after all.

Frannie paused in the entrance of the white-painted brick church less than a month after Jack had declared his love for her. She wore the gown he liked so much, the gown that carried memories that still could make her blush. Just as she'd predicted, it took a legion of people to help with the long satin train. Behind her, four of her nieces and nephews stood clutching the slippery fabric in determined little hands.

Ahead of her, Jillian was moving into the bridesmaids' place near the altar. She looked stunning in the sky blue tea-length gown Frannie had designed for her. Her blond head was bent and she was talking softly to Alexa, whom she cradled in her arms while the lacy white ruffles of the baby's gown spilled over her arm. Deirdre, halfway down the aisle, wore a matching style in palest pink, her long dark hair rippling around her as she slowly proceeded through the gathered crowd.

Now it was D.J.'s turn. She heard the electric whir of his wheelchair as he started down the aisle, and a lump came into her throat as his small hand reached into the basket secured to the chair and with jerky motions, scattered rose petals along the white runner between the pews. She'd been so touched when Jack had suggested that D.J. act as a flower bearer.

The music changed. As the notes of "Ode to Joy" swelled to a triumphant, lilting melody, she turned her head and smiled at her brother. Donald smiled back, offering her his arm, and together they started down the aisle.

As she took the first step, her gaze met Jack's. He stood near the minister, his friend Stu and her youngest brother, Billy, at his side. All three wore severe black tuxes. Jack towered over the other two men, looking even larger than usual in the dark color and her smile grew tender.

He smiled back. As she drew nearer, she could see the love in his eyes, the confident assurance that this was the day he'd waited for, the day he would make her his for the rest of their lives. He reached out a hand and drew her to his side as Donald relinquished her, and the marriage service began.

It was like a dream. Prompted by the calm, solemn voice of the minister, Jack spoke his pledge to her and received her vows in return. She handed her bouquet of fragrant orange blossoms to Dee and saw that the smaller woman had tears streaming down her face. Jillian leaned forward and blotted the tears with the edge of a cloth diaper she had hidden in the folds of the baby's gown.

They exchanged the rings they had chosen together. After a few more moments, the ceremony was over, and she heard the minister's voice. "You may kiss the bride."

Jack's big fingers took hold of the edges of the sheer veil and lifted it carefully up and back out of the way. His eyes were a brilliant silver and his Adam's apple bobbed as he swallowed. Gently, he slid his arms around her and pulled her to him, and she lifted her face for his kiss.

"My beautiful bride," he murmured when he lifted his head. "I love you, Frannie."

"I love you, too—Jack!" The end of the sentence was a gasp as he swung her into his arms. A ripple of laughter swept through their gathered families and friends as he held her high and turned to face everyone.

"Put me down!" she whispered in a low, insistent tone.

Chuckling, he shook his head, holding her high against his chest as he began to stride back up the aisle. "No way, Mrs. Ferris. Now that I've caught you for good, I'm going to carry you everywhere."

Warm amusement rose, and without thinking, she said, "In another seven months or so, I'm going to be so heavy you'll need a wheelbarrow to lug me around." Then her eyes grew big and she clapped a hand over her mouth. She'd just found out for sure yesterday and she'd planned to tell him in a few days, after the craziness that surrounded the wedding was over.

Jack's arms went rigid around her and he stopped dead in the middle of the church, pulling her even closer. His voice was strained. "Are you telling me—Frannie, are we going to have a baby?"

She nodded, smiling, knowing that he would be as thrilled with her news as she had been. "My wedding gift to you."

He bowed his head and touched his forehead to hers for a long moment, and when he slowly raised it again, there were tears glittering in his eyes. "We're going to have to celebrate an additional anniversary on our calendar. Because the day you walked into my office was the best moment of my life, the moment that led to all of these other miracles."

And as her husband began to move again, she relaxed,

safe in his embrace. He was right. Like it was yesterday, she remembered the first time their eyes had met.

The true miracle was that their lives were now joined forever.

* * * * *

Watch for Deirdre's sensuous love story by
Anne Marie Winston,

DEDICATED TO DEIRDRE,

coming February 1999 from Silhouette Desire.

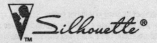

If you enjoyed what you just read,
then we've got an offer you can't resist!

Take 2 bestselling love stories FREE!

Plus get a FREE surprise gift!

Clip this page and mail it to Silhouette Reader Service™

IN U.S.A.	IN CANADA
3010 Walden Ave.	P.O. Box 609
P.O. Box 1867	Fort Erie, Ontario
Buffalo, N.Y. 14240-1867	L2A 5X3

YES! Please send me 2 free Silhouette Desire® novels and my free surprise gift. Then send me 6 brand-new novels every month, which I will receive months before they're available in stores. In the U.S.A., bill me at the bargain price of $3.12 plus 25¢ delivery per book and applicable sales tax, if any*. In Canada, bill me at the bargain price of $3.49 plus 25¢ delivery per book and applicable taxes**. That's the complete price and a savings of over 10% off the cover prices—what a great deal! I understand that accepting the 2 free books and gift places me under no obligation ever to buy any books. I can always return a shipment and cancel at any time. Even if I never buy another book from Silhouette, the 2 free books and gift are mine to keep forever. So why not take us up on our invitation. You'll be glad you did!

225 SEN CNFA
326 SEN CNFC

Name	(PLEASE PRINT)	
Address	Apt.#	
City	State/Prov.	Zip/Postal Code

* Terms and prices subject to change without notice. Sales tax applicable in N.Y.
** Canadian residents will be charged applicable provincial taxes and GST.
   All orders subject to approval. Offer limited to one per household.
   ® are registered trademarks of Harlequin Enterprises Limited.

DES99   ©1998 Harlequin Enterprises Limited

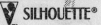
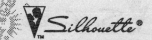

COMING NEXT MONTH

#1195 A KNIGHT IN RUSTY ARMOR—Dixie Browning
Man of the Month/The Lawless Heirs
When Travis Holiday found out he had a son, he realized it was time
to settle down—no more heroics! Then a long-haired goddess named
Ruanna Roberts was stranded in a storm, and Travis just had to save
her. But Ruanna was determined to rescue *Travis!* Could she crumble
the armor around his soul and claim his heart for her own...?

#1196 SOCIETY BRIDE—Elizabeth Bevarly
Fortune's Children: The Brides
Weeks away from a business marriage and Rene Riley was secluded
on a remote ranch with the man of her dreams! Though cowboy
Garrett Fortune defined unbridled passion, Rene was the only woman
he wanted. He just had to convince her that the only *partnership* she
was going to enter into was a marriage to him!

#1197 DEDICATED TO DEIRDRE—Anne Marie Winston
Butler County Brides
Ronan Sullivan and Deirdre Patten hadn't seen one another for years,
but one look and Deirdre knew the desire was still there. Ronan
needed a place to stay, and Deirdre had a room to rent. But opening
her home—and heart—to Ronan could prove very perilous indeed....

#1198 THE OUTLAW JESSE JAMES—Cindy Gerard
Outlaw Hearts
Rodeo was the only mistress in cowboy Jesse James's life. He liked
slow, hot seductions and short, fast goodbyes. Then Sloan Gantry
sashayed into his life. Could this sweet temptress convince the
"outlaw" that the only place to run was straight into her arms...?

#1199 SECRET DAD—Raye Morgan
Single mom Charlie Smith would do anything for her child—even
marry rugged mercenary Denver McCaine. She now had his protection,
but Charlie was wondering how much tender affection one woman
could take before dreams of happily-ever-after took hold of her wistful
heart....

#1200 LITTLE MISS INNOCENT?—Lori Foster
No matter what he did, Dr. Daniel Sawyer could not shake his desire
for Lace McGee. The sweet seductress had a tempting mouth and a will
of iron. But there was also uncertainty in Lace's eyes. Was it there to
drive him away—or did she hide an innocence he had never suspected?